THE LOGAN FILE

The Logan File has been closed for some time but its reopening triggers a story of blackmail in high places and international double-bluff, in which *glasnost* between East and West is held to grisly germ-warfare ransom.

Detective Chief Superintendent Simon Shard is sent to Germany to track down the blackmailers and his impossible boss Hedge is despatched after him. A desperate hunt across Europe leads Hedge to Moscow's Lubyanka as he discovers that old Nazis do die, but very slowly.

THE LOGAN FILE

THE LOGAN FILE

by
Philip McCutchan

Magna Large Print Books
Long Preston, North Yorkshire,
England.

British Library Cataloguing in Publication Data.

McCutchan, Philip
  The Logan File.

  A catalogue record for this book is
  available from the British Library

  ISBN 0-7505-1051-X

First published in Great Britain by Hodder & Stoughton, a
division of Hodder & Stoughton Ltd., 1991

Magna Large Print is an imprint of
Library Magna Books Ltd.
Printed and bound in Great Britain by
T.J. Press (Padstow) Ltd., Cornwall, PL28 8RW.

1

The killing had been very efficiently carried out: the men who had done it were expert, trained by other men who had learned their trade under men who in turn had been apprenticed to the Nazi thugs, the Gestapo, in Hitler's Germany of so many years ago.

Two men had been watching Frau Palmer's house: the visit to her house on the outskirts of Hanover by the Englishman, Detective Chief Superintendent Shard, had been known and since then the watch had been maintained very discreetly. The night of the killing the men had waited for all the lights to go out and after a safe interval had emerged from the cover of thickly-growing shrubs and undergrowth and had moved towards the back door of the house.

No word had been spoken: they each knew precisely the other's mind, knew precisely what to do.

They would not have long once the

burglar alarm went off—they knew that; they knew also that the alarm was too sophisticated for any intruder to throw it off the beam. So they moved very fast and they made no attempt to keep down the noise of their entry; the house was in any case well back from the road and standing in large grounds. A window was broken, and they went in like commandos as the alarm went off stridently. The servant was in bed, in a ground-floor room beyond the kitchen quarters. She came fearfully but bravely to the door and was gunned down in a blast from a sub-machinegun. The body fell without a sound and the men raced for the hall and the staircase. They pounded up the stairs, taking no notice of the continuing urgency of the alarm.

Trudi Palmer appeared in the doorway of her bedroom.

Without a word the men opened fire. Frau Palmer fell in a pool of blood like the servant. The men left immediately, moving swiftly down the stairs, out through the back door, through the garden behind the house and along a path through closely-set trees to a car waiting with two more men in it.

No-one saw them go. Burglar alarms

tended to go off for no apparent reason. That alarm had rung also in police HQ in Hanover: Trudi Palmer, born Trudi Strobel, now widowed by the Bader-Meinhoff gang, worked for the German security services. The police, at least, reacted, if too late.

Hedge, some days before, had given an involuntary shiver as he'd stepped out of the warm sanctity of the Foreign Office. It was a desperately cold night; and he felt furtive. He also looked it as he thrust his hands into the deep pockets of his dark blue greatcoat and settled his neck into the folds of a fawn-coloured muffler, cursing savagely beneath his breath at the telephone call that had come to his house while he had been breakfasting that morning.

Hedge's life was largely cloak-and-dagger; but he was not a field man and he much disliked being exposed. Those who ranked at only two removes from the Permanent Under-Secretary of State were not for exposure. Such was best left to the underlings.

But this time there had been, as Hedge had seen it, no option.

9

Muttering to himself, feeling aggrieved, Hedge moved on leaden feet towards the gloom of St James's Park, away from the lights of Horse Guards Parade and the Mall and Birdcage Walk. On such a night there were few people about. There was snow in the air, and a bitter wind that blew odd bits of paper, crisp packets and the like, around his feet. London was appalling these days, filthy with the indiscriminate castings of common people who all had more money than they had any right to. Foreigners as well, all nationalities polluting the capital. Hedge shivered again; it wasn't right. The shiver was one of intense distaste for the present day and its squalor. It's lack of respect, too.

Then he became aware that a man was emerging from behind a bush and was falling into step beside him.

When the call had come, Hedge had in fact been finishing his breakfast, a latish one and not frugal for a man well past middle age, a man with a not inconspicuous overhang to his stomach: porridge to keep the cold at bay, real Scots oatmeal that had simmered all night long on the Aga and had been brought to perfection by his housekeeper Mrs Millington; three rashers of bacon, three pork chipolatas, fried bread, two eggs, mushrooms sent in from the country—not the button variety, which were rubbery and without taste. All this followed by toast and marmalade and three cups of coffee, well sugared, these being accompanied by a hand-made cigarette purchased from an exclusive shop in the Burlington Arcade, lovingly made by the grandson of a man who in his time had made them for the Duke of Windsor when he had been the Prince of Wales.

Bliss; and not, so far as Hedge had been aware until now, to be followed by a busy day in Whitehall. Diplomatically, or at any rate security-wise, it had appeared, the last day or so, to have been the slack season, for which Hedge had been grateful. There had been a good deal of to-ing and fro-ing ever since Comrade Gorbachev had begun back in '89 to stir things up; the dismantling of the Berlin Wall, of the whole Iron Curtain, and the helter-skelter way in which the satellite countries had discarded communism—all that had led to immense difficulties one way and another while new alliances were sought and the whole business of frontiers and so on was sorted out and the thorny question of German reunification was raised time and again. Such would take time to bring about even if it was desirable: there were still the opposing interests of NATO and the Warsaw Pact; the two Germanies were still in opposing military camps. But these last few days...the season of goodwill and all that: Christmas was not far off, and the Head of Security, Hedge's immediate boss, had already gone to the country with his wife. When H of S was off the scene, Hedge took things a little more easily, though his staff didn't seem to think so. He made them, rather than himself, work a little harder, with longer hours. During this forthcoming afternoon, he would visit a massage establishment in Soho where he would find both relaxation and stimulation.

And then that wretched telephone call.

He heard the ring. Mrs Millington came in. He regarded her sourly; she had piano legs, cook's legs—not perhaps surprisingly since she was a cook. The caller, she said, was a lady.

'A Mrs Reilly-Jacobs, sir.'

'Oh, yes. Thank you, Mrs Millington. I'll take the call in here.'

Mrs Millington, all severe dress and sniff, for she suffered perennially from a nasty cold and catarrh, left the room and Hedge answered on an extension. 'Yes, Mrs Reilly-Jacobs?' Mae-Li Reilly-Jacobs was the wife of an assistant under-secretary in one of the Whitehall ministries, a man with whom Hedge had played the occasional round of golf. 'What can I do for you, dear lady?'

When his caller answered, Hedge felt sudden shock. 'You're not Mrs Reilly-Jacobs!'

'No.' The voice was not English; further than that, Hedge was unable to place it. 'But I think you must listen, Mr Hedge. It is important.' There was a pause. 'You are listening, yes?'

'Oh, very well, yes,' Hedge said, full of apprehension.

'I shall not speak on the phone,' the unknown woman said. 'You will come to meet me. This evening at six-thirty in St James's Park. At the eastern end of the pond with the ducks—you know? You will come alone. If you do not come alone there will be no contact, but the result will be unpleasant for you. You understand, yes? And in the meantime,

13

Mr Hedge, you will say nothing to anyone at all.'

'But—'

There was the sound of a cut-off. Hedge jiggled at the handset uselessly, and shook it, his face wobbling like a jelly. The voice had been an unpleasant one, and the acquired English accent had been common, not that of anyone whom Hedge would be likely to know socially. But she knew his name, knew his ex-directory telephone number—probably knew where he lived. There must have been a massive leak of security somewhere along the line. Hedge was supposed to be anonymous—he was, in fact, a hedge, a screen between H of S and ordinary people, the kind of buffer to protect the higher brass of the Establishment. It could be most serious if his cover was blown. And what, for heaven's sake, did the woman mean by the use of the phrase unpleasant *for him?* Hedge mopped at his face, which had begun to sweat. He lit another cigarette.

He drove to the Foreign Office. He enquired if Mr Shard was in. Detective Sergeant Kenwood, FO Special Branch, answered. 'He's in, sir. Do you wish to speak to him?'

'It doesn't matter,' Hedge said, and rang off. He bit his nails. He sat at his desk in agitation, a prey to his nerves. Should he, or should he not, confide in Simon Shard? Shard, detective chief superintendent ex the Yard and now Hedge's right-hand man, knew all the tricks of cloak-and-dagger. But the woman had known his telephone number and his name...she might get to know of other things, she might even have her spies inside the Foreign Office itself. No-one was safe these days, you couldn't trust anybody.

Hedge passed a wretched day, full of indecision and trepidation.

'Hedge,' the man said. 'As expected. And alone.' Hedge felt the muzzle of an automatic nudge his side through two layers of clothing. 'If you turn out to have company lurking it'll be just too bad.'

'What precisely do you mean?' Hedge quaked.

There was a harsh laugh. 'One guess.'

Hedge didn't press the point: really, the query had been unnecessary. The automatic had spoken for itself loud and clear. Hedge said, 'I was expecting a woman. Who are you?'

'Never mind who I am. The woman...she doesn't matter either. Walk along with me.'

'Where to?'

'Never mind where. Just keep with me.'

'Oh, very well.'

They moved on, down the side of the lake furthest from Birdcage Walk. Still there were a few people about. Hedge looked longingly towards his left, at the guardsroom of Wellington Barracks, with good, solid guardsmen on sentry duty, part of England's glory, men who represented safety and sanity in a threatening world. Why, oh why, had he not confided in Shard? But if he had, then he might well have been dead by now. Shard, like the policeman he was basically, would have insisted on providing cover, and, however distant, that cover might have registered with the man with the gun.

Hedge asked, 'What do you want of me?'

'Assistance.'

'I see. Er—can you be more precise?'

'I can. And soon, Hedge, I shall be.'

They moved on towards Buckingham Palace. Light snow began to fall, gently powdering the trees and bushes, gently powdering Hedge's greatcoat and muffler. The only sounds were those of traffic moving along the Mall and past the palace, to and from Victoria or the Admiralty Arch. Soon the snow would muffle them.

Hedge and his escort emerged from the park. 'Watch it,' the man said. 'Don't do anything I wouldn't like.' There was a short wait; then a big black car, a Volvo, slowed and pulled in towards the pavement. 'Get in,' the man said as another man beside the car's driver leaned back and pushed the rear near-side door open. 'Be quick about it.'

Hedge got in and was given a violent shove from behind, a shove that sent him head first into the well in rear of the driver's seat. The car moved back into the traffic; Hedge remained where he was, face down, held there by the foot of the man who had joined him in the park.

During the day there had been contact between Hedge and Shard, contact over matters far removed from the female who had disturbed Hedge's breakfast. Minor departmental matters in the main, a few ends to be cleared up before the advent of Christmas. Hedge had been tempted

17

to discuss his call and in resisting this temptation had become distrait and dithery, a prey to his nerves and his indecision. Later, Shard had cogitated: what was up with Hedge? There were no clues. But at one point, on entering Hedge's sanctum, he had heard Hedge on the telephone speaking to Mrs Reilly-Jacobs, a name known to Shard. Hedge had cut short the conversation rather obviously, and had looked flushed. Some clandestine affair in progress? Hedge was, and this Shard knew, a frustrated womaniser and Mrs Reilly-Jacobs was an attractive woman. Shard had seen photographs of her in society magazines, and in newspapers when she'd been at functions to do with her husband's ministry. Anyway, it was no business of Shard's, who believed in live and let live. But he found it hard to believe that anyone as attractive as Mae-Li Reilly-Jacobs would welcome the attentions of an elderly philanderer like Hedge, not exactly a sex symbol.

That night, Shard worked late. After Hedge had left his office, something had come in from Germany, from the British Embassy in Bonn. It had been urgent, and had needed Hedge's personal attention.

When Shard had used the security line to his house, Mrs Millington had said Mr Hedge had not returned. Not returned at all since leaving for the FO that morning. The time was now nine-thirty-four by Shard's watch. Mrs Millington, when asked, said that yes, it was unusual for Mr Hedge not to give her due warning that he wouldn't be in, or at least to telephone to say he'd been delayed unexpectedly. She'd had his dinner all ready for him and it was spoiling. Normally, he dined at eight-thirty sharp, a man of punctilious routine.

Feeling uneasy, Shard rang through to Beth, his wife, whom he'd called earlier to say he would be late home. It now looked, he said, as though he might stay at the FO all night. He knew Beth didn't like being alone in the house and he wasn't surprised when she said she'd ring her mother and see if she could come round. Mrs Micklem lived rather too close for Shard's liking. He made a wry face into the telephone and said that would be fine.

He wondered again about Mae-Li Reilly-Jacobs but decided that was too fanciful altogether.

After a very uncomfortable journey Hedge

was decanted into a garage, the door of which was shut behind him before he was permitted to emerge from constriction. There was a light in the ceiling but the garage was totally anonymous. Hedge was taken through a doorway into a big square hall with a number of other doors opening off. There was an atmosphere of money about. The floor was well-polished parquet and bore a number of expensive-looking rugs. When he was pushed into a drawing-room he found a lush carpet and what looked like genuine antiques. He had no idea where he was; in London or out of it? The drive had been a longish one.

He was told to sit down. He sat in a big armchair. He was watched by the two men from the car and by the man who had picked him up in St James's Park, who seemed to be the owner of the house. This man had put away his automatic. For the first time Hedge had a proper look at him. He was tall and well-dressed and he seemed to be a gentleman, which term Hedge would not have used for his companions, one of whom wore jeans and a T-shirt advertising a brand of lager. A lager lout? Hedge didn't like it, didn't like it at all. The third man was simply squalid, with a beer gut behind a cheap suit, thick lips and a nose that ran. The nose was bulbous with beer and the head was bald. Beneath it, the eyes were small and close-set. By Hedge's estimation, he was a thug. It was a curious set-up and a frightening one. People could be beaten up, killed. Bodies could be disposed of—there were so many methods. Dissolved in acid, buried in concrete and thrust beneath motorways under construction, thrown into deep water with heavy weights attached to the feet. Bodies were by no means indestructible.

But why should these people wish to kill him?

Perhaps they didn't.

Not if he co-operated?

But in what way? Hedge's mind, in the absence of any conversation initiated by the other parties, was running ahead of itself. Perhaps they had made a monumental mistake and it was not he they wanted. Hedge was Foreign Office, something very far removed from crime and criminals. Of the ordinary sort anyway.

The man, the original man, moved across the room and unlocked a tantalus from which he drew a decanter of whisky. He poured himself a generous shot and added water. No drinks were offered to his companions or to Hedge. Glass in hand, the man came back and stood looking down at his captive.

He was smiling now. Hedge licked at dry lips and asked a question.

'What is all this about? Surely you realise you're taking an immense risk in—in abducting anyone of my standing?'

'I think the risk is slight, Hedge.'

'Do you?'

'Yes.' The wretched man was smiling still, looking down sardonically at the seated Hedge. 'Largely because of your own character, I'd venture to say.'

'I'm afraid I don't follow you.' Hedge's tone was stiff.

'No? Then I'll try to explain, Hedge.' The man took another pull at the whisky and studied Hedge's face. He said, 'You are a vain and pompous man, Hedge. Conceited. You set a lot of store by your position in society. In the Foreign Office. You would not like scandal. And you are vulnerable. Vulnerable in a number of ways, one of them being Mrs Reilly-Jacobs.'

Hedge stared. 'What nonsense! What has she to do with me?'

22

There was a shrug. The man went on smiling but didn't utter. Then Hedge ticked over up to a point. He said, 'That telephone call. It was said to be Mrs Reilly-Jacobs on the line. Why?'

'Simply because we knew you would take the call. From a stranger, you might not have done. But, you see, you know Mrs Reilly-Jacobs.'

'Yes—'

'In a biblical sense, Hedge. If you follow.'

Hedge's cheeks were scarlet. 'What utter nonsense! What a thing to say! I've met the lady on a number of occasions and that is all. All, I tell you!'

'Possibly. But scandal can be so easily arranged. A word here and there, the odd hint, and the stage is set. The press would love it, Hedge. They would make mincemeat out of you...adultery with the wife of a fellow high-ranking civil servant. I would think about that if I were you, Hedge.'

'But—but—really, this is quite preposterous! There has been nothing—no opportunity—'

'That's not important. The damage would have been done irrevocably. And the result, Hedge? Think of it for yourself. You don't need me to spell it out, I know.'

Hedge sweated. He pulled out a handkerchief and mopped at his face. Such evil men, with such evil thoughts, such evil intentions to sully the name of a lady, not to mention his own reputation. And of course he could see it. An accusation of a clandestine affair that would receive the accolade of truth the moment it appeared in the newspapers. Dirt in Whitehall, and a man high up in FO Security involved. He would be forced to resign. He mopped again at his face, his thoughts racing. Could these wicked persons actually read his mind, could they by some evil chemistry have been party to his innermost thoughts, the thoughts he was forced to admit to himself that he'd had many times about Mae-Li Reilly-Jacobs, the dreadful fantasies that visited him so often, Mae-Li Reilly-Jacobs in an unclad state, Mae-Li Reilly-Jacobs enfolding him in her arms while his hand strayed...but of course they couldn't know that. (But they might, if they were as clever as they seemed to be, have known about his visits to the massage parlour in Soho, and that wouldn't go down very well either in FO circles.)

He said, 'In St James's Park I asked you what you wanted of me. You said you would soon be precise.'

'Yes. I shall be, Hedge. In the park I said we wanted your assistance. That's all.'

'Well?'

The man turned away and went back to the tantalus. He poured himself another whisky. Then he gestured to the man with the T-shirt and jeans. 'Set it up now.'

The T-shirted man left the room. Hedge sat and shook. Clearly, something nasty was on the way. The man was gone for around five minutes during which time no-one spoke. Hedge guessed they were leaving him to stew. The man came back with a video cassette. The other man, the thug with the bulbous running nose, sat on the arm of Hedge's chair and brought out a knife which he held against Hedge's throat. 'No tricks,' he said.

The television was switched on. After some preliminary flickers, the screen showed an airport, one that Hedge didn't recognise right off.

'Hanover in West Germany,' the original man said.

The scene shifted, showing a man getting into a car, presumably outside the airport. All Hedge saw was the back of the man, who looked elderly and wore a wide-brimmed hat and a cloak. The man was short and squarish. The scene shifted again, showing some buildings, and the car stopping outside a garage. The driver got out and opened the door for the elderly man with the hat and cloak. Now Hedge could see him full face. A kindly face, seamed with age, with humorous eyes and a friendly smile, a man who had been well known to him in years past and whom he had thought was dead.

'You recognise him,' the man stated as the projector was switched off and the lights came on again. 'You recognise Logan.'

Logan. Francis Edward Moncrieff Logan as he had been known to the British security services. But born Heinrich Helmut Schreuder in Potsdam, in the year 1910. Logan, man of many parts.

'Logan alias Schreuder is still alive, Hedge,' the man said. 'The film was shot very recently. At this moment, Logan is contemplating a trip into the German Democratic Republic.'

Logan. Hedge felt icy cold. Logan, whose kindly features were nothing but a front, a trap for the unwary, had been a time bomb.

He could become one again.

2

It was two hours late before Hedge was allowed to leave the house. The men were polite; would he like to be dropped handy for his home, or handy for the Foreign Office? Hedge opted for the latter; he had left his car there, and, urgently, he needed to study the back files, the computerised information on Logan to bring his memory up to date, even though there were aspects of Logan that in fact he knew he could never forget.

The Volvo dropped him in Whitehall and drove off fast, but not before Hedge had astutely made a note of its registration number. Walking fast for the FO he was admitted by the night security staff who were used to Mr Hedge appearing at odd hours. He enquired if by chance Mr Shard was in the building.

'He is, sir, yes.'

'Ah, good. Ask him to be so kind as to come immediately to my office.'

Hedge went upstairs in the lift and

28

walked through to his office suite. Hard on his heels came Simon Shard.

'I've been trying to get hold of you, Hedge—'

'Yes, yes, Shard. First things first.' Hedge knew that he had now to confide in Shard. This thing could not be swept under any carpets. 'I've been subjected to—to unpleasantness. I've been kidnapped.'

Shard lifted an eyebrow. 'They didn't keep you long, Hedge.'

'No, they didn't, but that's not the point.' Hedge shifted irritably in his chair behind his big desk. Shard was often too flippant for his liking, lacking in a decent respect, but the police were like that these days, not really knowing their proper place. 'The point is, I'm being threatened.'

Unbidden, Shard sat in an easy chair facing Hedge. 'You'd better explain fully, hadn't you?'

Hedge did. He started with the telephone call ostensibly from Mrs Reilly-Jacobs. Shard caught him up straight away. 'You should have told me, Hedge,' he said.

'Yes, I see that now. But I was threatened, you see, even at that stage. I decided not to risk anything.' Before Shard could catch him up again he launched

29

into his exposition of the kidnap. He told Shard what had been said about Mae-Li Reilly-Jacobs.

'Dirt,' Shard said. He looked hard into Hedge's eyes. 'No truth in it, I take it?'

Hedge answered snappishly, 'Of course there's not, what a thing to ask—typical police reaction.' He paused, seeing the sardonic look in Shard's eye. 'You do believe that, I hope?'

Shard nodded. 'Yes, I believe it. Go on, Hedge. What do they want?'

Hedge told him about Logan. Shard reacted. 'Logan,' he said. 'Now that's odd. What I had to report to you...that's about Logan too.'

Hedge looked alarmed. 'Coincidence?'

'Probably not. I've heard from the Bonn Embassy—the same as you've just told me. That Logan's alive and is about to cross into East Germany. If we take it he really is alive—'

'Oh, he is. They showed me a video.'

'Of Logan, recently?' Hedge nodded; Shard went on thoughtfully, 'A video. Why couldn't they have sent it to you? Less risky, I'd have thought. Total anonymity, no faces, no house interior to be described later.'

Hedge dabbed at his cheeks with his handkerchief. 'I think it was a case of—of personal impressment, if you follow. They *bullied* me, you know, Shard. It was more immediate than a video arriving out of the blue, I suppose. And they had to get their points across, of course.' Hedge paused. 'How long has it been known that Logan's alive, Shard?'

'A matter of a few days, that's all—'

'It should have been reported sooner.'

'Bonn wanted to be sure. They didn't want to jump any guns. Logan's been a long time dead. Or said to be dead.'

'But now that he's not—'

'Yes—now that he's not. He's hot, Hedge, very hot, even after all these years. That is, if he lands up in Moscow. History tells us quite a lot, you know. It tells us our hands, British hands, were not all that clean in our dealing with wartime Moscow—right?'

Hedge nodded glumly. A lot had indeed become known about Logan, who had been a double agent. Through Logan a good deal of false war information had been passed to Russia, much of it on behalf of Logan's other master, Adolf Hitler. The results of this chicanery had been fairly lethal for Russia and had led among other nastiness to greater Russian casualties during Hitler's march on Stalingrad than would otherwise have been the case. Even today, even with *glasnost,* Moscow would not be pleased with Britain if the truth came out, and Logan might have his own reasons for implicating Britain.

Shard asked, 'What do these people want with you, Hedge, in connection with Logan?'

Hedge was sweating again. He dabbed at his cheeks and there was a shake in his fingers that Shard noticed. He said, 'They want him, Shard. It seems they want him themselves.'

'What for? Did that emerge?'

'Not precisely, no. But we do know of Logan's strong Nazi sympathies—that is, we've come to know since the wartime days. At the time, of course, that wasn't known—'

'So you're saying there's a Nazi connection, Hedge?'

'Yes—no. A neo-Nazi perhaps. All this reunification business...it's only too likely a reunified Germany will throw up another Hitler. The Germans still have their dream, you know. Some new charismatic patriot—'

'Not Logan.'

'No. Logan's too old now. But—'

'You think these people are Nazi sympathisers, do you?'

Hedge hummed and ha'ed. 'I really don't know what to think. But there's a strong probability that's the case, though I—' He broke off. 'One thing that occurs to me is this: if they want Logan, why can't they get him themselves? Why get me to do it for them, Shard?'

'I'd guess they want to remain out of it. Clean hands and all that. They may not have much of an organisation for that sort of game. And they've got a hold on you. Mrs Reilly-Jacobs.'

'Oh, that's such rubbish.' Hedge said, and almost said a lot more before he decided not to: unless and until he was forced to he shrank from telling Shard about the real threat to his future, it was all too nasty.

Shard asked, 'Have you no clues at all as to these people's identity?'

'No. Except that I did hear one of them being addressed as Todd.'

'Todd?' Shard paused. 'Or Tod. One d.'

'Why do you say that, Shard?'

Shard shrugged. 'Just a nickname. They won't be fools, Hedge.'

'We'd better check it out in any case.' Hedge looked irritated at what he considered nit-picking. Shard asked if anything else at all had emerged.

'I took the Volvo's number,' Hedge said. 'I thought it advisable, you know.'

Shard said gravely, 'Good thinking, Hedge. What was the number?'

Hedge had already brought out his notebook. 'F 39 UCK,' he said.

There was a sense of humour around: but the men had taken a risk. As Shard remarked, no registration numbering committee would ever have passed such a combination of letters. Hedge angrily accepted that the number plates were false. He told Shard to send up the file on Logan alias Schreuder so that he could refresh his memory and then said that when that had been done Shard could go home.

'What about Logan, Hedge?'

'What about him?'

Shard said patiently, 'Since he's alive, we have to react, haven't we? Never mind your kidnappers, we don't want him within the Eastern Bloc, do we, and it's still an

Eastern Bloc of a sort—'

'Despite the freedoms—yes. Well, no. No, we don't. Really, Shard, I've had rather an upsetting night. After all, I'm no longer young, you know. I need some time...but I think you'd better alert the Bonn Embassy that—that we have the matter in mind and—and instructions will follow.'

'When?'

Hedge was looking distracted. 'When I've reported to the Head of Security, of course. I'll do that in the morning. Meanwhile there's no special urgency.'

'Isn't there? He's—'

'Kindly leave me to make the decisions, Shard. I am your superior officer, a fact that I shouldn't need to remind you of.'

Shard arranged for the software on Logan to be sent up to Hedge. Then he left the security section, picked up his car from the parking lot and drove home to Ealing. Beth was already in bed. As he made himself a sandwich and a cup of strong coffee laced with whisky, Shard could hear Mrs Micklem snoring in the spare bedroom. He tried to shut his ears to the sound but without much success;

Mrs Micklem's snores were as loud as her voice. He reflected that a detective chief superintendent in his middle thirties really shouldn't let himself be so bothered by a mother-in-law; but Mrs Micklem was a pervasive woman who had mentally never let her daughter go. Now it was the grandchild, young Stephen, aged three and a bit, who was in her web. If mother-in-law had her way, he'd be spoiled stupid. Already, war had been declared on that.

Shard went up to bed, got in carefully, trying not to wake Beth. He didn't sleep for a long while. Hedge was on his mind. Hedge, he was convinced, hadn't told him everything. And why did Hedge appear to see no need for hurry in regard to Logan? It would have been possible to have contacted the Head of Security at his home in the country, and Shard would have thought the re-emergence of Logan was big enough to rouse out the Prime Minister let alone a senior civil servant.

Hedge, he was convinced, was hiding something. And it seemed as though that something might well be personal. Not just Mrs Reilly-Jacobs, either.

In the Foreign Office, Hedge concentrated

on his task. More or less...he found his memory all too clear. Francis Edward Moncrieff Logan had been his *bête noir* years ago and it was shattering to discover that the man was still alive.

Hedge's thoughts went right back. Heinrich Helmut Schreuder, born in Potsdam in 1910 when Kaiser Wilhelm had been on the throne of Germany and King George V had been about to succeed as head of the British Empire, had been a soldier of fortune, with a dabbling hand in many enterprises, all of them shifty. He had spent a good deal of his time in Britain and had come to know the country and its people well. In Germany, he had been for some years a member of the Nazi Party and had become friendly with the Party leadership to the extent that Adolf Hitler had placed a good deal of trust in him. When war had broken out he had been in Britain and had been of immense and immediate use to the Fatherland as an agent; the Fatherland knew that already he had volunteered his services to the British, having neatly changed his identity to that of Logan with a past history to support it. The British security services, being in a state of flux, had failed to check his credentials as closely as they might have done; and in Germany he was known as a patriot, a good Nazi, and a man with very many contacts inside the British Isles.

Logan had become a double agent, a fact that the British authorities never did discover until after the war was over. He had passed invaluable information to his Berlin master and had thereby been responsible for very many British casualties. In the war's early stages, in the period of the "phony war", he had provided information that had led to the sinking by a German U-boat of the *Athenia* filled with women and children making for safety in the United States; similarly he had had a background hand in the penetration of the boom at Scapa Flow by Kapitanleutnant Prien, whose torpedoes had sunk the battleship *Royal Oak*.

However, it had been long after the war that Logan alias Schreuder had impinged upon Hedge. Logan had sought refuge in the Irish Republic, living there under yet another pseudonym. From the far west of Ireland, in Connemara, Logan had pulled many strings. He still had his contacts in Britain and in West Germany. Logan was a born manipulator, a born agent. He had that friendly manner, that kindly face. He had charm, and some very unexpected persons fell victim to it, Hedge being one.

Many years ago now. It had been back in the 'sixties, when Hedge had been a more junior, but up-and-coming, member of another Whitehall department—the Ministry of Defence. There had been information that Logan had needed; by this time Logan was engaged in the arms trade with an interest in nuclear weapons. He had world-wide connections and a lot of money behind him. Among the customers of his principals were Libya, Iran, Syria, China, and the USSR plus some South American countries.

Hedge had been remarkably naive, remarkably foolish. He had an expensive life-style, expensive tastes that his Whitehall salary did not meet. Champagne tastes with a gin income. He had taken Logan's money—had taken bribes. Certain information had been passed to Logan. Nothing, of course, that in Hedge's own view could have been prejudicial to the national security—Hedge had his standards—but which was useful to Logan's business interests. And, innocuous as it might all have been, Hedge, had anything ever emerged, would have faced charges under the Official Secrets Act, then disgrace, loss of pension rights, and a few years behind bars.

And still could.

Sitting at his desk, Hedge gave a shiver of fear. It was a nasty situation. And why was fresh pressure being placed upon him by way of false revelations about Mrs Reilly-Jacobs?

Why bother? They already had quite enough on him.

The one hope was that they simply didn't know about what had gone before. If that was so, then they had better not find out.

It was absolutely necessary to play along with them now. Absolutely essential.

But what was he to tell Shard? What was he to report to the Head of Security? Those wicked men had given him his instructions very clearly, and in basis they were simple enough. As he had already told Shard, they wanted Logan out from East Germany—or apprehended before he left the West—and then he was to be handed over to them. The second part was obviously the hard part. Not only hard to bring about, but very hard on Hedge personally: with Logan in their hands they would be dead sure to find out about the bribery, and then they would have Hedge right over a very nasty barrel.

So what was the answer?

If he didn't go along with them, scandal would break. And once the press had got onto that, there was no knowing what else they might dig up, how far back into Hedge's past they would go. And if he did go along with the kidnappers—though how he had no idea currently—his secret would be laid bare by Logan.

A prey to mounting terror, Hedge left his office suite and went down for his car. By now, it was the early hours.

That night he slept no more than did Simon Shard. When sleep did come, it was filled with nightmares about the Old Bailey, a bewigged judge making references to a highly-placed civil servant betraying the nation's trust, and then the horrible clang of a prison door.

Procrastination was perhaps the thing, a display of masterly inactivity. For now, anyway, Christmas was not far away...nothing ever did get done over

Christmas, everyone knew that, even villains. Christmas was all around Hedge: Mrs Millington had already decorated the house with expensive red-berried holly from Harrods, and—perhaps hopefully— mistletoe, plus a collection of tinselly stuff of various colours, little glittering red, green and blue balls and whatnot. A hideous bauble dangled over Hedge's mostly uneaten breakfast. Driving to the FO, Christmas was again evident, canned music playing "I'm dreaming of a white Christmas", depictions over the shops of Father Christmas driving his wretched sleigh along with more music, "Sleigh bells in the snow".

And snow fell: Christmas again. Hedge did not feel Christmassy. In his office, he rang down for Detective Chief Superintendent Shard. He had, he said, arrived at a decision: he would report formally to the Head of Security, telling him that the matter, the word from Bonn, was in hand.

'That's all?' Shard asked.

'Yes, Shard, it is.'

'And Bonn?'

'Bonn?'

'Where the report came from,' Shard said wearily.

'Yes, yes. Bonn.' Hedge frowned, tried to conceal the nervous twitch of his lips. 'I don't think there's any hurry, Shard. Not over the holiday, you know.'

'The message was urgent. From Bonn.'

'From Security, in Bonn.'

'Yes, Hedge.'

'Not from the Ambassador?'

'Not from the Ambassador, no, but—'

'Then I don't believe there *is* much urgency. We don't want to be a nuisance, Shard, upsetting—'

'Christmas?'

'Yes, exactly. A time of—of happiness and—'

'Peace and goodwill?'

'Yes, that's it, Shard. That's it precisely—'

'And in the meantime, Logan gets across to East Germany and possibly, eventually, to Moscow?'

Hedge shifted irritably. 'There is *glasnost*, Shard. Things have changed very considerably. I don't think we fear Russia any more. Why, there's religious freedom...they even, as I understand it, celebrate Christmas. They *enjoy* themselves.'

Shard's face was hard. 'You're gabbling, Hedge. With respect, you're talking nonsense.'

'Oh, really? I call that sheer impertinence and—'

'Look, Hedge. That message from Bonn was clear, distinct and quite obviously urgent. You can't just sit back over Christmas and pretend it didn't come. You'll have to inform H of S fully—and soonest possible. I don't see why you haven't done that already. Bonn will be bellyaching any minute now—'

'Bellyaching! Really, Shard, I do wish you'd keep your Scotland Yard expressions out of my hearing.' Hedge pushed at various items on his desk, his fingers shaking. What a confounded nuisance Shard could be at times, always so pushing and would-be dictatorial, often treating him as no better than a village idiot. 'In any case, what do you expect me to do about it, may I ask?'

'Instruct Bonn immediately to have Logan apprehended. Isn't that what your kidnappers wanted—to say nothing of what should be your duty, Hedge?' Shard paused. 'I have to ask, what more is there behind this?'

Hedge blustered. 'What the devil do you mean by that, Shard?'

'What I say. I get the impression you've

44

not come entirely clean. That you're hiding something.'

'Really, I—'

'And if that's the case, then I suggest you come out with it before you drop in too deep.'

'I am hiding nothing,' Hedge snapped. He drummed his fingers on his desk. 'Oh, very well then. I'll report to H of S that action's being taken on the Bonn message. And tell Bonn I'll be in touch when I've heard from H of S—who of course may feel the need to refer the whole matter to the assistant under-secretary.'

'More delay,' Shard said.

'It would be the usual procedure, Shard.'

Shard left Hedge to it. When he was alone, Hedge, with an obvious reluctance, took up his security line to the country home of the Head of Security. When told that H of S was not currently at home, Hedge gave a metaphorical sigh of relief. Surely, if Logan reached East Germany before he could physically be prevented from so doing, those ruffians could scarcely lay any blame upon himself?

Hedge tried to turn his mind to other matters.

Hedge's "other matters", mostly a load of departmental details, were interrupted.

Shard again.

'Yes, what is it, Shard?'

'Further word from Bonn,' Shard said.

'Oh, dear—'

'Logan. He's gone.'

Hedge's jaw dropped. 'Gone? What d'you mean, gone? Is he—'

'Flown, Hedge. He's now inside East Germany. Last seen in Magdeburg—'

'What a time to choose,' Hedge said dispiritedly. 'It's Christmas.'

'Very unfortunate,' Shard said. 'What are you going to do about it, Hedge?'

'I'll try H of S again.'

Hedge did so; H of S was still not at home. The matter now began to assume urgent proportions of a personal nature. Hedge hummed and ha'ed, shooed his secretary off the line when she rang, something about a memorandum that was overdue and was being chased by the Cabinet Office. Should he now act on his own initiative and refer the Bonn report to the assistant under-secretary, or should he sit on it a little longer, waiting for the Head of Security to return from wherever he had gone? It really was a problem. He was still dithering when his outside line rang. He answered it. He was expecting Mrs Millington to ring; she had a sick sister-in-law, widowed, and she had hinted at breakfast that she might have to leave Hedge to his own devices that night and possibly over the festive season, as she called it, as well. She would let him know as soon as possible.

It was not Mrs Millington.

'Hedge,' the voice said. It was not the woman this time; Hedge recognised the voice of the kidnapping house-owner of the previous night. 'By now, you'll know what's happened. About Logan.'

Hedge shook, his face whitened, but he said nothing.

'Are you hearing me, Hedge?'

He nodded into the telephone. 'Yes...'

'Get your skates on, Hedge. If you don't, you know what happens.'

In desperation, Hedge found his voice. 'It's not up to me, as I tried to tell you last night. Interpol—'

'Blarney, Hedge. You know that as well as I do. Get moving, or you're for the chop.'

The call was cut. Hedge trembled; he hadn't done what he should have done, got his secretary to alert Shard and have the call tapped. He had a button on his desk for precisely that purpose, a signal to his secretary that she would have understood and acted upon instantly. He had been so upset, too shaken to react. Shard would be blistering about that. He decided to say nothing yet to Shard. Instead, suddenly making up his mind, he rang his secretary and told her to pass to the assistant under-secretary that he wished humbly to have audience of him. Five minutes later the assistant under-secretary was on the line himself.

Hedge sat to attention before the telephone. 'Hedge here, Under-Secretary. I do apologise—'

'I haven't time to see you personally, Hedge, though I fully intended sending for you later. There's been a report from Bonn about a man called Logan—are you with me?'

'Er—yes, yes, Under-Secretary, I—'

'It's a very serious matter. I should have been informed immediately and I shall want your explanation as to why I was *not*. Logan is not on any account to be allowed to remain in East Germany, much less to enter the Soviet Union, but the extraction is to be done with the fullest discretion. It's vital that...certain past matters do not become known to the Kremlin.'

Hedge tried his best. 'But *glasnost*, Under-Secretary—'

'Bugger *glasnost*. When these past matters of security arose there was no *glasnost*, only Siberia and mental wards. And the Russians aren't basically all that far removed from those days even now, even with *glasnost* and what's the other thing—'

'*Perestroika*, Under-Secretary.'

'Yes. I suggest you get that man of yours—Shard, isn't it—into the field as fast as possible with orders to bring Logan out.'

'Yes, Under-Secretary,' Hedge said with a sinking heart. The wish of an assistant under-secretary, like that of the captain of a ship, was a command. The same principle applied to a suggestion. Shard had now to be faced. So had his own future.

Shard had been mentally prepared for orders to go out into the field. Unlike Hedge, his function was basically that of a field man, not that of a polisher of office chairs. He'd known that a pierhead jump would become inevitable as soon as Hedge overcame his curious reluctance to refer the matter to higher authority. Logan would never be left to the mercies of the Eastern Bloc. To Shard it was clear that Logan/Schreuder had not gone into East Germany of his own free will. He would not be easy to extract from determined captors. Shard had spent the morning reading up about Logan's past so far as it was known. Some of his war-time chicanery had been directed against Russia, the iron-hard Russia of Comrade Stalin. Russian memories were long, and Russia was still Russia whoever ruled it at any particular time. And revenge was still sweet. In Shard's view Logan could well be left to be dealt with by the Soviets, despatched to a well-deserved death, but of course that was not the way in which governments, or government departments anyway, worked.

The orders from Hedge, now that they had come, were for immediate action. Shard, who always kept a packed grip in his office, rang Beth.

'I don't know how long,' he said. 'But just don't worry about me if I don't contact.'

Beth, as ever, kept her voice level but Shard could sense the disappointment. 'Damn the FO,' she said. 'It's Christmas.'

'I know, darling. Try to explain to Stephen. I'll make it up another time.' He risked a query about Mrs Micklem. 'Your mother, Beth. Will she stay on?'

'You bet she will,' Beth said. She herself found that too much of her mother became something of a trial; Mrs Micklem was a perennial giver of unasked advice, especially about little Stephen. But Beth could cope; she always did. She'd married a copper with her eyes open, had known all about the periods, some of them lengthy, of grass widowhood.

Shard checked his grip and rang down for a car to take him to Heathrow and a BA flight to Hanover, where the villains' video as observed by Hedge had shown the thick back of Logan.

3

There was the usual Christmas-time crush and bustle at Heathrow but the Foreign Office on duty bound could not be denied and Shard had been fitted in aboard a flight for Hanover without any overt difficulty. Waiting in the VIP lounge, and then during the short flight to Hanover, Shard reflected on Logan and his likely value to the Kremlin. It must in fact be virtually nil; the war had been a long time over. Logan's secrets wouldn't be worth a kick in the backside now; it had to be the revenge motive.

Or had it?

Logan wouldn't be all that big a fish to the Russians. Hedge had gone on about *glasnost*, and certainly *glasnost* was now a fact of life to be considered in any dealings with the Kremlin. The Russian leadership, the new leadership, would surely not be wanting to rake up the long dead past, to exacerbate the West unnecessarily?

Maybe it wasn't the Russians who

wanted Logan, but if not them, then who?

On another tack, another line of thought, had Logan still a value in Whitehall, other than the negative value of not being allowed to open his mouth in the East? He had been presumed dead for so many years now; his sudden re-emergence would probably have put a few cats among the pigeons. Shard, by training a policeman, tended to be cynical about not only the Foreign Office but about all government departments. Whitehall was a strange place at times, so were its denizens, and they tended to present a united front, closing in around their own when there was difficulty. Except, of course, when the knives were out in internecine warfare and somebody might see a chance of kicking somebody else in the teeth.

That might or might not apply in the case of Logan.

And Hedge?

Shard still believed Hedge had not told him all he should have told him.

Shard had contacts in Hanover and on arrival he took a taxi to a house on the southern outskirts. A servant answered his ring. Frau Palmer, she said, was in. Who should she say was asking for her?

'Just an old friend,' Shard said. 'An old friend of her husband.' He spoke in German. The servant said she would convey the message and he must wait.

He waited just inside the hall. After a minute a middle-aged woman came out. Her eyes lit up when she saw him and she came forward with outstretched arms. 'Simon,' she said, smiling. 'It has been a long time—I am glad to see you, so glad.'

He bent and kissed her. Frau Palmer dismissed the servant and led the way into a drawing-room. An old friend of Shard's, Detective Chief Inspector Neil Palmer of Scotland Yard had married Trudi Strobel when he had been on secondment to Interpol in Bonn. Within two years of their marriage he had been gunned down by terrorists—the Bader-Meinhoff gang. Trudi Strobel had been a civilian worker in Interpol; she had carried on her work after marriage. She had never been to England and after widowhood she had still carried on her work. Now, as Shard knew, she freelanced under cover for Interpol, an adviser on terrorism and security. It was an unusual appointment; Trudi Palmer was an unusual woman; and still very attractive.

Shard was offered a glass of wine; he accepted. Rung for, the servant came back with a bottle of Reisling. Shard and Trudi Palmer talked of old times, asking how each had made out in the intervening years. It was very obvious that Trudi missed Neil Palmer a great deal. She would never, she said vehemently, remarry.

'But it is not for this that you have come, Simon.'

He acknowledged it. 'No. I believe perhaps you can help me.'

'This is—official?'

'It's official duty,' he said. 'But I'm here unofficially. You know what my work is now, don't you?'

She nodded.

'I'm here on a mission that has to remain under cover. There's a man who's wanted back in Britain.'

'Yes? And this man's name?'

'Heinrich Helmut Schreuder, alias Logan, Francis Edward Moncrieff Logan. He was born in Potsdam in 1910. And I see from your expression, Trudi, that you don't know of him.'

'No,' she said. 'I do not. Can you tell me any more, Simon?'

He said, 'He was dead but is no longer—he was believed dead—'

'But he is after all alive.'

'Yes. And has been observed here in Hanover. At the airport, getting into a car.'

'When was this, Simon?'

He shrugged; Hedge hadn't known that. 'I don't know. But I'd guess recently.'

'And after that?'

'He crossed into East Germany, route and destination—final destination—not known. But he was seen yesterday in Magdeburg.'

The woman frowned. 'You say, Simon, his final destination. Do you mean Russia, Moscow perhaps?'

'Yes. That's on the cards. If that's where he's bound, well, he has to be intercepted.' He paused. 'You've heard nothing of him at all?'

'No, I have not. Tell me, Simon, is this man a terrorist?'

'Not so far as is known. This doesn't concern such outfits as Bader-Meinhoff, the IRA and so on—nothing like that. And you're going to say that your work's terrorism pure and simple. So you wouldn't necessarily know.'

'Yes, that is right. I am sorry to say—I am sorry not to be of help.' She wrinkled her nose attractively. 'However, there is perhaps some little help I can give. I have a contact in Magdeburg, an East German who can be fully trusted and I shall give you his address. And in the meantime I shall see what I can find out about this Logan, or Schreuder, and I shall pass the information to my good friend in Magdeburg.'

'It'll be a great help, Trudi. Thank you.'

She smiled and gave him her hand. 'It is nothing. For old times' sake, as you say. You were a good friend to Neil. So often he spoke of you.'

Hedge had gone home in a fractious mood. Desperately worried about his situation vis-à-vis the wretched Logan, he was now also faced with domestic upset. Mrs Millington had rung—and so upset by this time was Hedge that he had had a tap put on her call before he'd answered, which had made him look a fool—she had rung to say that her sister-in-law was very poorly, had taken a turn for the worse in fact, and she would have to go to her aid. Blood, she had said, was thicker than water, and although Hedge would have disputed any blood relationship with a sister-in-law he had been forced to accept her dictum. He found it a trifle thick, coming as it did over Christmas.

Hedge, these days, was a bachelor of a sort. His wife had walked out on him, taking with her the furniture that was hers, having it loaded clandestinely into a pantechnicon while he was slaving away in the Foreign Office. A couple of years later she had died, which he thought served her right. Mrs Millington, who had not been in the least surprised when the mistress had done her flit, now looked after Hedge totally. Except, it seemed, when her sister-in-law called.

During the day, after Shard's departure into the field, Hedge had had a check put on anyone called Todd with two ds and Tod with one d. There had been quite a number of Todds and a couple of Tods but none of them had fitted in the remotest degree and Hedge had felt baulked, terribly frustrated. Tod had obviously been some sort of nickname only, as Shard had said. Hedge was also chagrined about F 39

UCK. That had made him look a fool too. But of course he hadn't got Shard's mind, the mind of a common policeman, the sort of mind that saw dirt in everything.

And there had been no clues as to who "they" were, the despicable villains who had kidnapped him. Shard had been no help over that either. As Hedge banged about in his kitchen, looking for food and saucepans—he could have gone out for a meal, of course, but that would have been risky, such dreadful things happened these days and he might be got at—he reflected that Shard was a horrible man.

Across London, Mrs Micklem thought the same. She had never liked her son-in-law, who on occasions had been formidable, just as though she was the interfering sort; he had told her off and she hadn't liked it, but something had kept her back from hasty retorts. Simon Shard let it be known that he was master in his own house and she knew she had to watch her step thereafter.

Sitting before the gas fire she said, 'Christmas on our own, Beth. Or so it seems.'

'Yes, it does.'

59

'Of course you'll miss Simon. But it's nice to be like old times, isn't it? Only of course without your father now.'

Beth nodded, staring into the fire. Simon had helped to put up the Christmas decorations, holly and ivy—brought up in the country as a child, he always insisted on ivy—and all the rest. Now, it all looked rather despondent. Mrs Micklem went on, 'It's such a shame for Stevie. People are very thoughtless.'

'It's not exactly Simon's fault, mother.'

Mrs Micklem's voice was patient. 'No, dear. I never said it was. I was thinking of the people who—who sent him away at this time of the year.' She paused, looking critically at her daughter. 'You know, Beth dear, I often think you're rather too *defensive*. You don't like things being said...you jump to conclusions. It's as though you think I'm—'

'All right, mother.'

'There you go again, don't you see? All I—'

Beth got to her feet. 'Let's leave it, mother, shall we?'

Mrs Micklem noted the way her daughter's hands were clenched into fists, noted the anger in her face. 'All right, dear,' she

60

said peaceably, 'there's no need to fly off the handle with your mother. We only live once, you know, and it's Christmas.' She bent and picked Stephen off the rug, where he'd been playing happily with some Lego. 'Come and give granny a nice, big kiss, darling,' she said. 'If you haven't got your daddy, there's always granny.' She added sharply, 'Don't struggle so. You hurt granny.'

Legs and arms flew in her lap. 'I'd rather have daddy than you. I don't like you.'

Mrs Micklem flushed. 'Well I never, there's gratitude for you.' Beth had gone out of the room now. Mrs Micklem took the opportunity of giving the boy a smack.

Shard had rung for a taxi from Trudi Palmer's house. While he waited for its arrival, Trudi used the telephone herself, speaking to someone in Hanover. There would be a seat for Shard, she said, on the Lufthansa flight leaving Hanover airport at 1630 for Berlin. Shard had seen no point in remaining in Hanover, trying to pick up leads that were probably not there. In Hanover he'd had hopes of positive information from Trudi Palmer. Now he had to move on, get close up

61

behind Logan before worse happened. Or possibly before Hedge in London made some sort of cock-up that would leave his field man dangerously exposed. Such had happened in the past and Shard was always wary that it might happen again.

On arrival he checked into a West Berlin hotel, then called at the British Consulate-General, by appointment made on the telephone from Trudi Palmer's house. He had an interview with a second secretary on secondment from the Bonn Embassy, asking for certain assurances while he was in East Germany.

He asked if there was any knowledge of Logan in West Berlin.

There was not. 'Of course, we're in possession of the known facts, Mr Shard—that this man Logan has surfaced. And really that's all we do know. Also that he appears to be in Magdeburg.'

'You've had no instructions?'

The second secretary shook his head. 'Not a thing, no. We understand it's being left to you.'

'Yes. You don't know of any associates of Logan's?'

'No, I'm sorry, we don't.'

'Yet the original report came from your people in Bonn.'

'Well, yes, it did. I agree. It came to us anonymously as I believe was reported to Whitehall. A telephone call, but naturally it had to be acted upon.'

'How,' Shard asked sardonically, 'did you act on it? By informing Whitehall—just that?'

'Yes. There was nothing else to be done, was there, Mr Shard?'

Shard thought: perhaps not. When dead, Logan hadn't even had a grave that might otherwise have borne investigation. According to the stored and retrieved information, he'd suffered a particularly nasty kind of death: going round a steelworks in West Germany, a place where his principals had a financial interest and as a result so had he, he had managed to fall headlong into a vat or tub or whatever of molten metal and that had been that. There had been nothing left, or nothing that had been getatable when the metal had cooled. Obviously the man who'd fallen in couldn't have been Logan, and that was another mystery in itself. Unless his resurrection was all eyewash. Shard would have come to the conclusion that it was indeed eyewash if it hadn't been for the undoubted fact of the kidnapping and threatening of Hedge.

When Shard got back to his hotel room he found he'd had a visitor.

One of the day's disturbing events that had so upset Hedge had been his summons early that afternoon to the presence of the assistant under-secretary of state, a man ranking in the FO hierarchy, the permanent Civil Service hierarchy, only one degree below God. Hedge had practically genuflected when bidden to sit down.

'I'm not pleased, my dear Hedge. Far from it. Time's been wasted, you must realise that.'

'I'm sorry, Under-Secretary. If only my chief had been available when needed...'

'I've not brought you along to listen to excuses, Hedge. You're not some junior clerk. There are occasions when you have to use your own initiative. This was one of them. You failed to approach the mark expected of you.' The assistant under-secretary was a tall man with the face and voice of authority. Had he chosen another career he might have been an admiral or a general. Hedge quaked but tried not to show it. He protested that he had done his best in the circumstances but had not found much support; he had Shard in mind when he said that, but was not given the chance to elaborate. The assistant under-secretary gave a grunt and said that obviously his best was not good enough.

And then Hedge was subjected to an interrogation.

A very full exposition of the telephone call to his home had been demanded and there were questions pertinently asked about Mrs Reilly-Jacobs. Hedge was closely questioned as to why he had not made an immediate report and his mumbled explanations about risks and the good name of a lady hadn't been satisfactorily received and Hedge had the nasty feeling that the name of the lady had been noted for reference in the future. He told the whole story of St James's Park and the unknown house and about Todd or Tod. And F 39 UCK came up once again, causing the assistant under-secretary to utter a loud snort of derision.

Logan, the cause of the whole thing, was not gone into in much detail at that stage; but when Hedge had been dismissed from the presence the closed telephone lines became almost red-hot. Home Office, Ministry of Defence, Treasury, Cabinet Office, Department of the Environment, even the Ag and Fish. Francis Edward Moncrieff Logan had had many contacts in high places. Hedge hadn't been the only one. By tea-time that day, when the various personal secretaries were filling the ministerial cups, there was a very great deal of concern about Logan and his whereabouts, and much bated breath as Whitehall awaited the next move.

The evidence that awaited Shard in his hotel bedroom was pretty clear. To him, at any rate. Small things had been shifted in the drawers into which he had unpacked his grip. Nothing much; but enough. The hotel bedroom staff could be presumed not to ferret around in residents' drawers, unless of course with evil intent. Other things; a picture on one wall that he had very slightly tilted was now tilted the other way, as though someone had been, perhaps, looking for a concealed wall safe. Shard, who had a photographic mind, always made a point of noting the position of everything in a hotel bedroom.

And in the past that had paid off. This time he noted something else: perfume, rather stronger than would be permitted to a chambermaid.

The someone who had been in his room was a woman. She was unlikely to call again, he believed.

Shard turned in after a final drink from the bedroom's well-stocked bar. Falling asleep quickly, he dreamed of home. Ealing, the neat house and garden, the large mortgage, Beth, Stephen and mother-in-law.

Also Hedge.

It was not nightmares about Mrs Micklem or Hedge that brought him awake suddenly, awake and watchful but silent and motionless. There had been a click, very faint, as of the door to the corridor shutting behind an intruder. But the room was very dark and he saw no-one. He heard nothing further; but a sixth sense told him that someone was there. The someone was keeping very still, no doubt assuring himself that Shard was asleep still.

After a while he smelled the perfume. There was the faint creak of a floorboard. By this time Shard had slid a hand beneath his pillow and had his automatic ready.

With his free hand he reached out and flicked the bedside light on.

He saw the woman, young, little more than a girl; registered that she was pretty. She stood petrified, staring back at him, not speaking. He was covering her with the automatic, and was looking as if he might use it.

He asked a question.

'Who are you, and what do you want?'

She was trembling. She didn't look like any sneak thief or any undercover woman. No-one, Shard thought, would ever have employed her as such. She was, he believed, freelancing; but what at?

'Out with it,' he said brusquely. 'I may use this.' He gave the automatic a jerk. 'What's a young woman like you doing bursting into hotel bedrooms at night, h'm?'

She licked at her lips. When she spoke it was in English, halting and heavily accented. She was German presumably. She said, 'I am sorry. It is the wrong room.' She apologised again, and moved for the door.

'Just a minute,' Shard said. Swiftly he was out of bed, putting himself between the girl and the door. 'Something tells me it's the right room. I think you've been here earlier this evening. Right?'

'Oh no, no—'

'I beg to differ, young lady. People don't normally sneak in dead quiet, and move around the way you just did, trying to make no sound—not if they come in thinking at first the room's the right one. So I think you'd better start telling the truth. Unless you want me to ring for the management.'

She didn't like that. 'No,' she said breathlessly. 'Please, no.'

'All right. Start talking. To begin with, what's your name? I'm assuming you know mine?'

She didn't answer that. She said, 'I am Gerda Schmidt. You know?'

He shook his head. 'No. Should I?'

'It was possible.'

'I see,' Shard said. He didn't at all. 'Now kindly answer my second question: do you know my name?'

'Oh yes,' she said. 'It is Herr Shard.'

He grinned tightly, still standing over her with the automatic. 'Right room after all. Now I think we're going to have a more comfortable talk. Move over towards the window, Fräulein Schmidt. There's a chair. Sit in it.' He reached behind himself and locked the door.

The Hanover police, having reacted to the alarm ringing from the house of Trudi Palmer, now very dead, had at once informed Bonn. The result of their report reached London and drew Hedge, just an hour after the killing, from his bed. His telephone, the security line, brought the voice of the assistant under-secretary.

'Yes, Under-Secretary?'

There was trouble in Hanover. 'I presume you're familiar with the name of Trudi Palmer, German widow of—'

'Yes, Under-Secretary—'

'Good. She's been murdered.' Details were gone into. 'Something else: Shard had called on her in the early afternoon—yesterday afternoon now. I see a connection with Logan/Schreuder. Shard'll have to be informed and you'll have to pull out all the stops now. I'm on my way to the FO. I'll expect you to get there before me.'

'Oh, dear—yes, Under-Secretary, of course.'

The call was cut. Hedge, muttering to himself, lumbered out of bed, retrieved his

70

teeth from a tumbler by his bedside, thrust them into his mouth, had a hasty wash, got dressed and went down for his car. He detested driving at night; headlights coming towards him blinded him and threw him totally off balance, but duty was duty and everyone, of course, knew what the assistant under-secretary of state was like But driving through the snowy night for the Foreign Office, Hedge wondered what on God's earth he was expected to do about a murder in West Germany. In all conscience, he'd scarcely recovered from his own kidnapping. And as for pulling out all the stops...Shard, already in the field and on the job, was just about the only stop available to him so far as he could see. He certainly didn't intend to go into the field himself.

The assistant under-secretary permitting, that was.

Any suggestions along those particular lines would have to be fought off. Somehow.

4

'Now,' Shard said. 'You'd better talk, Fräulein Schmidt. I know you've been in this room. How about starting by telling me what you were looking for?'

The girl was crying now. Shard blew out a long breath and asked, 'Do you know why I've come to Germany, Fräulein?'

She nodded. 'That is why I came to your room, Herr Shard.'

'Go on.'

There was no hesitation now. It seemed to come in a rush. 'I wished to—to find out things, you know? I wished to find out what you knew, and I searched for documents, anything that you might have brought that would help me. I knew you were here in West Berlin—'

'How did you know that?' he asked.

'I was told.'

'By whom?'

She didn't answer straight away. Then, with reluctance, she said, 'A friend in the office of the British Consul-General.'

'Is that so?' This, Shard did not like. 'Is this friend British, Fräulein, or German?'

'German,' she said. 'A West German—'

'Of course. What else did this friend tell you?'

'That you had come to look for my grandfather, whose name is Schreuder.'

'In there,' the man with the gun had said two days earlier in the hallway of a house on the fringe of countryside close to Magdeburg. Nudging his captive in the back with the gun barrel, he urged him towards a doorway at the end of the hall. Reaching past the elderly man, he pushed the door open. Steep stone steps loomed in the backglow of an electric light that had come on as the door was pushed open. The gun nudged again, and the man went down. As he reached the bottom the man with the gun spoke again. 'Our friends in Moscow will come for you shortly. I do not know when. Here you will be safe.' There was a harsh laugh, then the door was banged shut. There was the sound of bolts being drawn across, then, after retreating footsteps from above, silence.

The man, whose name was Schreuder alias Logan, felt his way around the cellar

73

in the pitch darkness, his breath, the breath of a terrible fear, coming in short gasps. He stumbled into something and went headlong, hurting his knee as he fell, and gashing a hand on a sliver of wood.

Getting to his feet, he found that he had stumbled over a raised plank—three plants that formed a seat or a bed. On this, he sat, putting his head in his hands. The last two days had been a time of nightmare. The snatch had been very professionally done. He had known that the Kremlin wanted him, had known this for some years past. But he had felt safe; safe after the sudden spread of freedom and after the fortuitous accident, which had not been precisely an accident at all, had resulted in his being presumed dead. That had cost him a lot of money; the fact that it had also cost a man's life was not important to Logan. His own safety, his own anonymity, was. But in the end they had got him, using his grand-daughter as the bait. Logan, not a man given to love of his fellow men, was devoted to his grand-daughter, Gerda Schmidt.

He had had the message; the message that she needed him, that she was sick in her shared flat in West Berlin. The message had come by telephone, from her co-tenant; or so it had said. Logan had found no reason to doubt its authenticity. He had started on the journey, leaving, or so he had intended, for Berlin via the Hanover airport. But at Hanover he had been apprehended by three men and hustled into a car and driven away. After leaving the concourse, blinds had been drawn over the car's windows and Logan himself had been forced down onto the floor in the back of the car. He could guess where he was being taken. The drive was a long one. A very long one, taken very fast. Logan, in the totally altered political climate, knew there would be little difficulty with frontiers.

Logan knew other things: he knew exactly why he was wanted, why he had been wanted for so long, in the Kremlin.

It was for what lay in his mind, the secrets of the past years, both British and German. In the war and since. The past lingered, it did not die, and many of its secrets had a relevance to the present day. But there was another consideration as well. An old man now, a disillusioned one, one who had for many years considered himself hard done by, a bitter man, Logan had one last big job lined up. A massive threat to Britain and all Europe, a threat that when it came to fruition would spread fast. And the time, the time of fruition, was about to come. The Soviets had been a little late in that respect.

Word of the time of fruition had reached Whitehall later in the morning of the sudden call to Hedge from the assistant under-secretary propelling him out of his bed. It came in the form of a letter posted three days before in the small West German town of Rinteln not far from Minden where there was a British army garrison. The letter was accompanied by a sheaf of closely-typed documentation, apparently scientific stuff. It was addressed to the Under-Secretary of State for Foreign Affairs, with copies to the Home Office, the Department of Health, and the Ministry of Agriculture, Fisheries and Food.

The detail was formidable and intricate; the purport of it was frankly terrifying.

A meeting of the Cabinet was called as a matter of urgency. Later, Hedge was sent for by God himself—the Permanent Under-Secretary, not his deputy.

'Your man Shard, Hedge. Any results?'

'Not as yet, Under-Secretary. It's early days.'

'I'm afraid we haven't many days left. Where is Shard now?'

'In West Germany, Under-Secretary, that's all I know. Shard has carte blanche to act and move—'

'Yes, yes.' The Under-Secretary of State was clearly a very worried man. 'You have no other word of Logan, Hedge?'

'I'm sorry to say not, Under-Secretary—'

'We have. We have this.' He pushed a typed paper across his desk towards Hedge. 'This is an extract, a summary of what's been received from Logan—obviously, posted before his disappearance. Read it—and hold onto your hat.'

Hedge read. The paper was short and precise, right to the point. Logan had with his scientific associates developed a vaccine of a violently vicious nature. This vaccine when injected into animals produced rabies. Not, according to Logan's summary, ordinary rabies. The vaccine enormously cut the incubation period so that an animal coming into contact with an infected animal—or a human bitten by an infected animal—would develop the disease within a matter of days.

Hedge, his mouth hanging open, looked up and was about to utter when the Under-Secretary cut in on him. 'Read on, Hedge.'

Hedge did so. He read that some thirty thousand animals, cats and dogs and rats mainly, plus some foxes and bats, had already been injected in well hidden compounds spread throughout Western Europe from the north of West Germany, down through France and Spain and into Italy. Also in the British Isles.

Hedge looked up glassily. 'Where on earth...'

'So far as this country's concerned, probably the remoter areas of the north. Also Wales perhaps. Of course, they'll be looked for. All police forces on immediate alert. But when they're found, what then? A vet's nightmare, Hedge—'

'It could be bluff, Under-Secretary.' Hedge put the document down with a shaking hand.

'Yes, it could be, certainly. But we have to take it very seriously all the same until we know different. The Ministry's veterinaries aren't committing themselves yet. They know nothing whatever about this new strain. They, too, tend towards the bluff theory. They say the disease as at present known wouldn't spread with anything remotely like the speed claimed in these papers—I understand it would normally take some months—but of course a new strain could make hay of that.' The Under-Secretary passed a hand over his face, looking harassed and uncertain. 'We'll know quite soon, possibly. Thirty thousand animals when released—which they're going to do at some unspecified date—the situation could become desperate within a matter of weeks if what these papers say is true.'

Hedge asked in perplexity, 'Why is Logan doing this, Under-Secretary? Do we know? What does he expect to gain?'

For answer the Under-Ssecretary passed across another document. This was Logan's own original message, typed on a separate sheet of paper, brief and to the point like the summary of the rabies threat. Logan, it seemed, was out for a big killing and his demands were going to shake Whitehall rigid. Logan/Schreuder was still a convinced Nazi. Herr Hitler, the paper said, had been right in his aims. There was still a very large if elderly number of the Nazi old guard alive in both West

79

and East Germany, men who had served their Führer in the Party hierarchy and in such honoured military arms as the Waffen SS, Germany's elite. And the Soviet Union—and never mind *glasnost* which, Logan wrote, was an irrelevance that would one day pass—Russia was still the enemy that had to be eradicated. And now was the time. With *glasnost* and *perestroika* and the hand of peace being offered around the world by the Kremlin, with the Russian masses tasting freedom for the first time in their existence, with most of the satellite countries having rejected communism, Russia was softening up. The withdrawal of missiles, the lifting of the Iron Curtain...if the West should strike now, there would be much success. A sudden nuclear blow, the sending off of the Trident missiles from the submerged submarines and a simultaneous air and land strike by the combined forces of NATO would hit with devastating effect against a Union of Soviet Socialist Republics that was facing a high degree of disintegration already. The trouble still continuing in Armenia, the state of civil war in Azerbaijan, unrest in many other places, the people defying the Russian Army, defying high-ranking Party officials sent in from Moscow.

'So—'

'So, Hedge, the West is going to be coerced into support for Logan's schemes. The West is going to be coerced into a sudden strike against Russia, without any formal declaration of war. A blitzkrieg. Like Adolf Hitler. And somebody like Adolf Hitler, no doubt, will rise again—possibly in a reunified Germany.'

Hedge stared. 'In the world as it now is...all the fading away of communism rendering all that sort of thing quite unnecessary even if... Logan must be crazy, Under-Secretary!'

'Stark, raving mad would be a more fitting description.'

Hedge brought out a handkerchief and wiped at his cheeks.

'Of course we won't concede. But even if we did, the whole thing would be impossible without America. How would Logan propose to get round that, Under-Secretary?'

There was a shrug. 'Don't ask me. He doesn't go into that. There's nothing about rabies being released in the USA—it would probably be impractical...unless a large amount of the vaccine could be imported through some South American state. We all know how easy it is to get drugs into the USA, cocaine and so on, from South America. So perhaps that's yet to come—the threat to America. Or perhaps—conjecture again—perhaps Logan reasons that once Europe was involved, America would be forced to join in for her own protection. Just to make a thorough job of it.' The Under-Secretary leaned forward and jabbed a gold ballpoint towards Hedge. 'Don't forget, Hedge, there are a number of influential senators in Congress who'd like nothing better than to obliterate the Soviet Union even now, even after all the doves of peace. We have some similar lunatics here in Britain. They may be difficult to restrain—once the rabid animals are on the point of release!'

Hedge had gone on, before being dismissed from the presence, to ask if the Under-Secretary saw some connection between Logan's threat and his being taken into East Germany.

The answer to that had been yes. The men from Moscow would want Logan in person, if it was to be assumed that the threat had leaked to the Kremlin. And if it had, the Under-Secretary said, then no-one could predict what might happen.

'But the threat would surely be blown in advance in that case, Under-Secretary?'

'Well—yes, it would. But Russia might decide to strike first. Frankly, whatever the Russian leadership says in public, there's not much real trust accorded the West in some Eastern quarters. And so many of our own politicians are unreliable, to use no stronger word.' Having come out with that, the Under-Secretary showed embarrassment. 'That's to go no further than this room, Hedge,' he said.

'Why, of course, Under-Secretary, you may rely upon me to respect a confidence.' Hedge sounded unctuous; he did not know precisely what had made the Under-Secretary utter his comment, his indiscreet —for a civil servant—comment. But he did know Logan; he had had good cause to. And he didn't doubt for one moment that others in high places, higher places than his own, had been suborned over past years by Logan. In present circumstances that could weigh. Heavily and dangerously. It occurred to Hedge—it had already occurred in fact—that his own kidnappers of recent date might be acting on behalf of those

83

highly-placed persons, fearful now that Lodge was known to be alive after all.

As this thought struck Hedge, a related thought came into the mind of the Under-Secretary. 'Those men, Hedge, the ones who seized you—'

'Yes, Under-Secretary?'

'It's now even more important than ever that *they* don't get their hands on Logan. I understood they tried to force you into delivering Logan to them?'

'Yes, that is so, Under-Secretary, but of course I would never—'

'Of course not, that goes without saying. But if Logan's found you'll have to be quick off the mark. Or Shard will.'

'Yes, Under-Secretary.' Very quick indeed. If Logan was apprehended and not handed over, Hedge was due for the chop from the villains. He didn't doubt their efficiency. And what about a freed Logan opening his mouth? At that dreadful moment an almost overwhelming desire came to Hedge, urging him to make a clean breast and get the past off his back once and for all. But the urge was not quite overwhelming enough; much danger lay that way as well.

Before being dismissed, Hedge faced

another bombshell. Logan had at all costs to be found, the Under-Secretary said. 'Shard on his own is not enough, Hedge, and I don't want our part in this to be, shall I say, taken over by the Yard or anyone else. You must take personal charge. You must get out into the field yourself.' He smiled. 'I'm sure you'll welcome the change, won't you?'

Shard had talked to the girl Gerda Schmidt into the small hours. She had not in fact seen her grandfather for some time and now she was blaming herself for her neglect of an old man, the more so as she had herself been the unwitting vehicle leading to his disappearance. She had never known that the grandfather she knew as Heinrich Schreuder was known also as Logan or that he had been a double agent acting in the German interest during the war. She did know about his Nazi connections, the men of the old guard who revered Adolf Hitler still. She did not herself, she said, subscribe to those views. She had no interest in politics and no party affiliations. She believed simply in peace.

Before going back to her flat, she told Shard something that interested him.

She said, 'I know one of grandfather's friends, an old man who was a member of the Hitler Youth and then joined the Waffen SS and fought against the Russians.'

'Yes, Fräulein?'

'His name is Wolfgang Brosak. There is talk about him that I have heard. He is one who wishes to re-establish the German Reich as it was under Hitler, one who hates the Russians as does my grandfather for the defeat of the armies marching on Stalingrad and Moscow so many years ago. That is something they cannot ever forgive or forget, I think. It is all so stupid now.' She paused, her face troubled with the silliness of old men. 'Herr Brosack lives in Lower Saxony, in Rinteln—'

'He's retired now?'

'No, he is some years younger than grandfather—he is old, yes, but he is a scientist and he has a laboratory in which he works still.'

Gerda gave him the address, saying that it was unlikely Herr Brosack would have any knowledge of her grandfather's current whereabouts but he might be worth a visit on the off-chance.

Worth a deviation? Shard decided not.

Logan himself might be well on his way into the Soviet Union. The faster Shard got to Magdeburg now, the better.

He had two hours' sleep; then his telephone burred, bringing him awake on the instant. He was required urgently in the Consulate-General.

When he got there, there had been a call from Hedge.

5

Hedge, shattered by the mere thought of going out into the field, had stammered and stuttered out his excuses to the Under-Secretary. He was no longer young; his field experience was not of recent date; he would be rusty. And so on and so on. He did not of course go into the real reasons: to go into the field would be *infra dig* for a man of his seniority; it would be very uncomfortable; and he did not wish to be too far from the hub of events since he had his position and his future to think about if those vile kidnappers should go into their promised action against him. Also, in the field the actual physical dangers were immense and at any moment one might get a shot in the back.

But it was no use: the Under-Secretary was adamant. And the sooner Hedge got off his backside and his office chair, the better. Yes, the Foreign Secretary himself would be informed of Hedge's self-sacrifice in the interest of his duty to his Monarch.

If Hedge saved the day, then there would be a good deal of kudos in it, which Hedge interpreted as nothing less than a CBE. Stretching the imagination, he could even see a K somewhere along the line. That sugared the pill.

He went home, home without benefit of Mrs Millington, and packed his essentials. Changes of underwear; socks, vests, pants, handkerchiefs...a flask of brandy, very good Champagne brandy to ward off chills and calm nerves. It was, after all, Christmas. Mrs Millington's attempts at decoration were all around him. He felt nostalgic about them now, wishing he could remain with them instead of gallivanting around Germany or wherever.

Christmas. Hedge thought vengefully that it was because of Christmas that the Under-Secretary of State was sending him into the field. There was no-one else available.

He had no idea where to start. Shard was the field man, the one who knew where he was going. Shard was used to it. Hedge was well aware that things were very different now from when he had last been out on actual operations. The world moved so much faster now, and one was no longer dealing with gentlemen, persons who spoke one's own language and who *understood*. Once, even one's adversaries—even foreigners—had had savvy.

Hedge decided to telephone Shard. If he was anywhere near a telephone.

The message left by Hedge had been to tell Shard to ring him back soonest possible at his home number. Using the security line, Shard did so.

Hedge's voice was uncertain. He sounded rattled, very badly rattled indeed. He told Shard that he was being sent out to co-ordinate the search for and apprehension of Logan.

'I don't know where to begin,' he said irritably.

Shard felt inclined to say, for God's sake stay in London.

'What?' Hedge asked, 'do you advise?'

'Make your HQ here in the Consulate,' Shard said. 'Then I'll know where to contact you.'

'Oh—yes, of course. You don't think... anything more active?'

'No, Hedge.'

The sheer relief in Hedge's voice was almost tangible. 'You're sure?'

'I'm absolutely positive, Hedge. You'll be far more use if you don't move around.' Like a blue-arsed fly, Shard was tempted to add. He resisted the temptation and Hedge went on to say that he would be available at any time if Shard wished to consult him.

'It's great to know that, Hedge,' Shard said. 'In the meantime, are there any further developments?'

'I was coming to that,' Hedge said, and passed the word about the threatened release of the rabid animals.

Rabid animals, and a new vaccine, a new and very virulent strain of one of the world's worst diseases. Gerda Schmidt had given Shard the name and address of a man who had known Schreuder, a man who was a convinced Nazi, a supporter of the notions of dead Adolf Hitler. A scientist, with a laboratory in Rinteln.

That deviation was going to be worth his while after all.

Shard made arrangements for a seat to be provided on the next flight out of Tempelhof for Hanover, back on his tracks. And a car to meet him at the airport. A British Army car for preference;

he might need some unofficial military support.

By 1030 hours that day he was being driven out of Hanover, south-west along the autobahn for the small town of Rinteln.

In the UK the alert was on now.

All police forces had been notified and there was a nationwide search in progress for the animal compounds. The ground search was being aided by helicopters. As yet, nothing had been said publicly; the press was currently in ignorance of the facts. A meeting of the Cabinet, hastily called together, discussed the issues. No-one knew what to suggest, other than that the infected animals be found and destroyed without delay. There was demurrence from the Home Secretary as to destruction; there would be protests from the animal rights people.

'We need to be extremely careful,' he warned.

His point was taken. Wholesale destruction of cats and dogs would be a wicked scandal in the eyes of many people, not only the eyes of the animal rights activists. That was, unless the public was informed of the threat.

The Home Secretary didn't like that one, either. He was, he reminded the anxious faces, responsible for law and order. Law and order might break down if the public knew what it faced.

'You can't have it *both* ways, Walter,' the Prime Minister said, fluffing at her hair-do.

They all agreed on that. One seldom disagreed with Mrs Heffer. But no-one put forward a solution. The PM pointed out that it might not be long before the other side, the Logan faction, released it all to the press anyway. While the Cabinet was deliberating, news came: from the Commissioner of the Metropolitan Police. Barts Hospital had reported a child of seven, not expected to live. The culprit, a Rottweiler, had already been shot after biting the little girl six weeks or so before.

After that news the mood of the Cabinet grew more sombre, even though the police did not connect the solitary case with the larger threat in any way. Before the meeting broke up, there was more news, this time from the Home Office—a report from Inverness of a helicopter sighting of what appeared to be an animal compound nestling in a remote glen in Sutherland. The helicopter had gone low and had hovered. There had been a lot of snow but a large number of dogs had been seen, running about in circles and barking ferociously, and the police spotter had believed he had seen some of them foaming at the mouth though he couldn't be sure. What he was sure of had been a kilted figure drinking from a bottle, presumably whisky, and waving a fist at the helicopter. The Scottish Office was asking for instructions. This thereupon fell into the province of the Home Secretary, who faced an immediate dilemma. Did you send in men, with veterinary advice, to make a ground capture? Were you justified in asking the police to risk a fearful disease? Or did you attack with guns and nets and whatnot, or with gas canisters dropped from the air, and kill the dogs and possibly their guarding Scot?

The Home Secretary temporised, unwilling to commit himself just yet. He said, 'A closer and more positive look, I think. The animals could turn out to be merely sheepdogs, collies, perfectly healthy, and the man a shepherd.'

There were no reports from other areas. The rabid animals had obviously been very well hidden away. If they existed at all. It might be wishful thinking but the Cabinet comforted itself by putting it on record that they believed the threat to be nothing more than bluff.

Yet the nagging worry was there. From that time on, none of them would approach a dog without terrible fear. And pussy, too, would find his or her nose out of joint. Cats indeed were especially dangerous. But their biggest worry was rats. The winter had until now been mild, with little rain, and it had followed a period of summer drought and intense heat. Rats had proliferated and had become predatory and fierce in their search for food. And mice, of course, were everywhere. Also, dogs had fleas.

But of course it hadn't happened yet.

Checks had been put on all the official establishments that worked under government licence on research into rabies: the Centre for Applied Microbiology at Porton Down near Salisbury; the Public Health Service Laboratory in Colindale in north London; the Central Veterinary Laboratory in Weybridge; and an Essex-based pharmaceutical firm.

All were satisfied that they had not been

penetrated or their work compromised in any way. Nothing had been stolen. All this was by way of routine enquiry: there had in fact been no suggestion in any of Logan's documents that any British source had been used.

And all the establishments were sceptical of Logan's claims. However, they did admit the possibility, the faint possibility because science was always coming up with something new, that a discovery could have been made by ill-disposed persons. Similar indications came in later from establishments on the Continent—France, Germany, Scandinavia, Spain, Italy, Austria—after the Prime Minister had spoken personally on the telephone to the various heads of government overseas. The American President was also contacted; and during the early evening of what was to become known as Day One, an urgent message came in from Washington to the effect that a noted veterinary researcher of unimpeachable reputation had reported having stumbled accidentally on a strain of rabies that *could* produce the results claimed by Logan. He had found no antidote.

Now the threat had to be taken for real.

Later still that evening, a Cabinet minister who had been present at that morning's meeting committed suicide. He had taken a massive overdose of sleeping pills after having drunk half a bottle of whisky, single malt at that, and had gone into a coma. He had died in hospital. His widow told the police that he had received a telephone call and had immediately left the house without telling her who the caller had been.

She said, 'There was a big car, a Volvo, outside—a little way down the road. I watched my husband, you see. He spoke to someone in the car and then came back. He looked...very shaken. I didn't ask any questions. You don't, you know. You mustn't pry.'

She was asked the colour of the car.

'Black,' she said. No, she hadn't got the number, the car was too far away. The number, the assistant under-secretary at the Foreign Office reflected when the report reached him, would almost certainly not have been F 39 UCK. They wouldn't have risked that little joke twice. But he believed there could have been a connection with what had happened to Hedge. Shaking his head ruefully, the assistant under-secretary took up his telephone and spoke to a certain rather shadowy department of state. Suicides had reasons. Suicides of ministers of the crown after receiving suspect telephone calls leading them to hasty visits to black Volvos may well have been caused by something rather nasty. It was, as he said to the man he had called, none of his direct business but the deceased minister's background might bear investigation. Further investigation, that was: obviously, he would have passed the security checks in the past. But you never knew.

Rinteln was a sleepy town, very clean like all German towns, none of the filth and debris chucked about by the unsalubrious British while on holiday. It lay across the banks of the River Weser—the River Weser deep and wide where, at Hamelin not so far away, the Pied Piper had lured the children from their homes. Shard's driver pointed out the British Military Hospital on the outskirts of the town. From the air, he said, the buildings could be seen to have been constructed in the shape of a swastika, emblem of Nazi

Germany—the place had been built as a German military hospital before the war. Now the ownership had changed. Shard, as if by way of conversation, had got the army driver, a corporal of the Royal Corps of Transport attached to the hospital, onto medical subjects and had asked if rabies was a particular problem to the army, such as would obviously not be the case in the British Isles with its quarantine laws and its protective seas.

'I'm no medic,' the corporal answered. 'But there've been several cases that I know of. In fact a mate of mine...he got bitten and didn't report it soon enough. Wasn't quite a bite really, just a sort of graze. The medics reckoned it was the dog's saliva, got an entry. Poor bloke was dead a couple of weeks later.'

Shard nodded thoughtfully. 'Who deals with rabies cases, do you know?'

'It'd be the medical consultant, Lieutenant-Colonel Shelton. Normally, that is. But he's off on Christmas leave. Major Bruce, he's standing in.' The corporal glanced sideways. 'Got a special interest in rabies, have you, sir?'

Shard gave a non-committal shrug. 'Just general interest, that's all. The EEC's

99

always talking about opening up the frontiers. I just hope they don't open them up to rabies.'

Major Bruce might be worth bearing in mind. There was a possibility that he might know of Wolfgang Brosak, scientist with a laboratory in Rinteln. Of course, there was nothing so far positively to connect Brosak with rabies, but at this stage of the game anything might prove useful.

No time like the present. Shard said, 'I'd like to make my number with the military. Drop me off here at the hospital, would you?'

There was a lengthy wait in reception. Shard had given his name only, no other details at all. Major Bruce was busy: he had a clinic after his ward round. Shard read the airmail editions of the London newspapers. There was nothing about the scare as reported by Hedge, nothing about Logan of course. And nothing about the suicide of a government minister, news of which had not as yet reached Shard either.

When at last Major Bruce appeared, looking around him with raised eyebrows for his visitor, Shard made himself known. Major Bruce was a short, square man with a brisk manner, wearing army uniform beneath a white coat. Shard had still given only his name, but Bruce, looking him up and down, said, 'You look like a policeman.'

Shard grinned. 'A good diagnosis, doctor. May we have a word in private?'

Major Bruce looked at his watch. 'A quick one.'

'I'm sorry to be a nuisance,' Shard said.

'Oh, you're not. I've time for a coffee break. Come along to my office.'

Shard followed the doctor along a corridor and into a small room. Bruce waved him to a chair. He sat, and the major, taking up a telephone, asked for two coffees to be sent in. He then said, 'Well, what's this all about?'

Shard produced his Foreign Office identification. Bruce studied the card. 'Detective Chief Superintendent, attached FO. Well, well! Somebody here a suspected spy, or what?'

'Not that,' Shard said. 'I'm sorry, Major, but I'm not authorised to say any more than that—'

The doctor waved a hand. 'Oh, that's all right, I understand. But I imagine you can tell me what you want of *me* in particular rather than the CO?'

Shard said, 'This is just an off-chance. I'm wondering if you happen to know a man, a scientist, named Wolfgang Brosak. He has a laboratory here in Rinteln—'

'Correct—and yes, I do know him. I know him very well. I've had him in for a consultation just recently. In the interest of saving a life...wouldn't touch the little bugger with a barge-pole otherwise. What's your interest in him?'

Shard said, 'Once again, I can't be precise. But may I ask you one thing: in what connection did you call him in? I mean—what particular case?'

'Hydrophobia,' Bruce answered shortly. 'Rabies. Brosak's an expert on rabies. That apart, he gives me the creeps. He's an out-and-out Nazi. Makes no secret of his admiration of Hitler and all he stood for. Refers to him as his Führer, a real bloody heel-clicker. Loathes us British...but he's a conceited sod and can't resist giving advice. Besides which, he's good at his job, very knowledgeable, very.' Bruce gave him a penetrating look. 'Now, tell me if you will—where do I come in?'

Shard said, 'You've already told me I look like a policeman. Brosak could come to the same conclusion. Which means, I need cover. You see, I want words with him.'

'I see. And our conversation's to be regarded as confidential?'

'Very much so, if you don't mind, Major.'

'Of course. Sealed lips. But what kind of cover can I give you that would pass muster? How's your medical knowledge?'

Shard smiled. 'Non-existent, I'm afraid.'

'H'm. In that case I can't pass you off as a visiting consultant. So now let's think.' Bruce frowned in thought. 'How about a man from the D of H, come over to discuss rabies and—'

'Rabies must not be mentioned, Major. Not on any account at all.'

'This grows curiouser and curiouser! Never mind that, though. I'll not pry. But I think the D of H is the best best. Rats, don't you know. I've been reading about a kind of rat plague currently in UK. Not just in the newspapers—we medics get an infernal amount of bumph to read from the ministry. You've come to talk about rats and how best to deal with an inundation. Brosak's got a whole menagerie of rats, mainly for experimental

103

purposes of course, but also because rats are another of his interests. Being a rat himself, you see.' Bruce grinned without humour.

Shard said, 'That seems as good as anything, I suppose.' He added, 'As a matter of interest, how come Brosak's admitted to a British military establishment, seeing that he's such a convinced Nazi?'

Bruce shrugged. 'Germany's the host country, my dear chap, and we're not at war. Besides, this is a hospital, not the headquarters of BAOR. All sorts of weirdos gain admittance—you may have noticed!' Suddenly he grinned again. 'Sorry, I didn't really mean to be personal.'

Shard said, 'I've been called worse in my time, Major. And you've been a big help, bigger than you realise.'

Bruce nodded. 'When it all comes out, I'll be in there for my OBE. Meanwhile, I'll give you some documentation about rats.' He pulled a sheet of paper from a drawer and began writing. The coffee came, and was welcome.

Hedge, co-ordinating in the Consulate-General in West Berlin, took a telephone call from the assistant under-secretary of state after which he metaphorically bit his fingernails to the quicks. A suicide, and a black Volvo. Two and two had been put together. Had Hedge anything to add to his statement about the kidnap?

'No, Under-Secretary. And I really must point out that there are a number of black Volvos in London—'

'Yes, there are, I agree, Hedge. It may be nothing but coincidence.'

'Yes,' Hedge said eagerly. 'That's it, coincidence, Under-Secretary.'

'On the other hand, there could be a link. I'm having that possibility explored.'

'I see, Under-Secretary. Er...may I ask by whom?'

A grunt of irritation came along the line from Whitehall. 'Do you need to ask, Hedge?'

That was all. The call was cut. Hedge was terrified. Of course he had had no need to ask his question; it was just that he had hoped against hope...the people to whom the assistant under-secretary had referred so obliquely didn't court the light of day. They were ferrets with evil minds, so-and-sos whose sole object in life was to burrow about in people's private lives and expose them to criticism and worse. Far worse. And if they were now to investigate a ministerial suicide, then all manner of things could come out. Hedge believed in fact that the black Volvo was no coincidence at all. And those wretched men who had kidnapped him and uttered threats very probably had something on the dead minister as well. He could so easily have been another victim of Logan's wiles and bribery. In the past no doubt, but those evil ferrets made the past their business. Logan, alive again, was lethal. He had to be found.

No, he hadn't. *Found, he would talk.* The two dreadful stools loomed again. Logan really had to die. Hedge shied from the thought, for he was no man of action. But if someone else killed Logan—

Who?

Shard. But it was highly doubtful if Shard would do that off his own bat. And certainly he, Hedge, couldn't order him to. Or even ask him to. Damn Shard's wretched conscience, damn his integrity! There were times when you simply couldn't afford too many of the niceties.

But if only Shard would at least get in

touch, then something might perhaps be worked out.

Hedge sat and trembled. It was all most unfortunate, so inconsiderate of that minister to commit suicide. Not the thing at Christmas. After a while Hedge found he could sit no longer in the office provided for him as co-ordinator of the Logan hunt. It was too nerve-racking, waiting for nemesis. If Shard rang it would be a pity to miss him but Hedge decided to risk that rather than go quietly mad with the strain of waiting and doing nothing. Hedge also found it very wearing trying to look busy. He left like a pool of nothingness in the midst of bustle. He missed his comfortable London routine. Here in the Consulate-General his position in the hierarchy was a shade uncertain.

He left his office, telling his allotted secretary that he had an appointment and would return in an hour's time. He went out into the street. He wandered along the Kurfurstendam, among the crowds. West Berlin had a festive air; after all, Germany was the home of Father Christmas, sleighs and reindeer, Christmas trees and all that. If Queen Victoria hadn't married good Prince Albert, the British would probably never have had Christmas at all as they had come to know it.

Hedge went into a large store: he ought to buy something to take back for Mrs Millington for Christmas, though he believed it would in fact be well after the holiday before he got back into his congenial Whitehall billet. He spoke in English to a shop assistant, seeking her advice as to headscarves—Mrs Millington was addicted to such, hideous things. So doing he was approached by a small boy, pugnacious but tearful.

'You're a Brit,' the boy said nasally, staring at Hedge hard.

The boy was obviously American. *'British,'* Hedge said. 'Most certainly I am. You don't think I'm a—well, never mind that. Why do you ask?'

'I've lost mom,' the boy said, his lower lip trembling. 'And I guess I don't speak German. My dad's a soldier,' he added helpfully.

'Really. Well, I don't see how I can help. Why not go—'

'My dad's a general.'

Hedge gave a start. A general, even an American one, was a general. He enquired the boy's name; it was that of the supremo of NATO. Hedge said, 'Oh, dear. But in that case he won't be hard to find, I imagine.' Later, he would have a good deal to say about security or the lack of it. The supremo's family should not be at large without a plain-clothes escort. West Berlin held all manner of desperadoes, terrorists and such, including the ubiquitous IRA. It was his bounden duty to act as escort himself, protect young life, young *brass* life, at least until mom was located. The child's mother might be anywhere; the store was the biggest in all Berlin, putting Harrods to shame sizewise. The best thing to do would be to take the wretched boy to the Consulate-General and contact NATO HQ in order to off-load him.

Importantly, Hedge said, 'Come with me.'

'Where to?'

'Somewhere safe. Where I can contact your father.'

Suddenly the boy, obviously sensibly brought up, looked suspicious. 'Say,' he said, 'you're not a nutter, are you?'

Hedge bridled and went a deeper shade of red. 'Well! What *cheek! What* a thing to say! I must say I'm very surprised at a general's son saying such a nasty thing.'

'Well, gee, I guess I'm sorry. But I've been warned—'

'Then why approach me, a total stranger, in the first place?' Hedge snapped.

The boy didn't answer that directly. He said, 'Take me to Santa Claus—'

'Father Christmas.'

'Okay, Father Christmas. Mom was going to. She might be there.'

Hedge let out a breath of exasperation. Father Christmas was not much in his line. He was half inclined to deposit the child in the care of the store manager or someone, but so many people couldn't be trusted these days and the store people were Germans and the father was the supremo and he himself was a highly-placed civil servant. Noblesse oblige in a sense, or anyway the upper classes helping one another out. If the Americans had an upper class. 'Oh, very well,' he said.

'Then I can tell him I'm lost and he'll find mom.'

'Tell who?' Hedge asked distractedly.

The boy stared. 'Santa Claus, of course.'

'Father Christmas. Yes, I see.' Hedge found the grotto where Father Christmas was doling out presents and dandling small children on his knee, speaking to them in German. Father Christmas looked genuinely old, scarcely needed the disguise of the beard, though of course a beard was statutory. Hedge briefly caught the eye of Father Christmas and was jolted by a sudden memory from the past. Though he saw nothing familiar in the bearded, fake bearded, face he was electrified when the old man spoke to the child next in line for his attentions. Hedge had always prided himself on his ability to remember and recognise a voice.

He had no doubts as to this one.

Father Christmas was Logan.

6

The day became a fraught one. The boy
was a frightful encumbrance and remained
so until Hedge had reached the Consulate-
General and handed him over to a minor
official with instructions to contact his
parents. The boy had not after all sought
the assistance of Father Christmas in
locating mom, perhaps thinking him more
of a nutter than Hedge, or perhaps just
over-awed by the beard and the sheer age.
Logan, of course, would be very old now,
eightyish.

Hedge spoke to the Consul-General,
Rufus Bland. Bland was naturally in the
picture as to Logan and the reasons for
Hedge having been foisted on him. Bland,
though polite, considered Hedge an old
woman, no adornment to the FO at all.
Hedge told him with much excitement that
he had seen Logan.

'You can't have,' Bland said.

'But I tell you—'

'It's known positively that Logan was

seen in Magdeburg. Is it likely—I ask you, Hedge—that he'd come back to West Germany, West Berlin in particular, and set up his face in public as Father Christmas of all things? He's in no need of a job, I imagine—'

Hedge said patiently, 'I admit a degree of unlikelihood. But people are unpredictable. I'm quite *certain* I recognised the voice. *Quite* certain.'

'I can't really accept that as evidence, Hedge. Did you not physically recognise the man?'

'No, I didn't. He'd naturally have altered—much aged since I was last—er—in contact with him. But the voice...I'm asking you to contact my man Shard, get him back here immediately.'

'All right, now look, Hedge.' Rufus Bland sat forward in his chair, elbows on the desk in front of him, 'if you're so certain—bear in mind that he may have recognised *you*—'

'Oh no. I'm positive he did not. There was no reaction at all.'

'But if he *did,* he's likely to scarper—if it's really Logan. I suggest the man's investigated, even brought in if you like, before he has a chance to vanish again.

We'll probably be made to look prize idiots to the German authorities, but I suppose I can't disregard what you think you've seen.'

Hedge said, 'I prefer Shard to deal with this. It's his job.'

'But Shard's not here.'

'I'm aware of that, Bland. I've already asked you to contact him and order him back.' Hedge added, 'I'd do so myself only I don't know where he can be contacted—I do know he's gone to somewhere in Rinteln but that's all.'

'Then how do you expect *me* to find him, for heaven's sake?'

Hedge said, 'You people have your avenues. I'm unaccustomed to—to Germany and its ways. And I say again, there's to be no arrest until Shard gets here.'

The Consul-General shook his head, utterly baffled by Hedge.

Hedge was in a fair way to baffling himself, his mind in a whirl. He was feeling his age. He had been precipitate in reporting his sighting of Logan to that fool Bland, whom he regarded as an upstart. Rufus Bland was not of the old school, not of a *public* school. For years now the FO had been recruiting from the wrong sort, the wrong class. Bland dressed badly, his clothes far too casual, like his manner, no respect for his elders. A gentleman would have done up his collar button when speaking to anyone like Hedge, tightened his tie, which in Bland's case was a revolting one of lurid stripes. But much more importantly, Hedge had blundered. His sense of duty had made him report what he believed to be the face of Logan, but he should have for his own sake refrained, and probably would have done had he not feared that it might have come out if Logan was captured and then said he *had* recognised Hedge, though in fact Hedge was quite certain he had not.

But so much the better if he'd kept quiet and just tried to contact Shard. He might have been able to work things out with Shard.

In the meantime he might manage some sleuthing of his own. When the store closed, he might be able to tail Father Christmas. Yes, that would really be the thing to do. It would not come amiss to have a private word with Logan, try to sort out some of the past. There would be pressures that could be put on Logan—Logan himself wasn't the only one who could put on pressures—Logan wouldn't want to be apprehended by the British authorities. A deal might be struck. Mightn't it?

Risky, of course. But other things were risky too. Hedge had a need now to act positively.

This he would do. Back in his office he looked at his watch. Plenty of time before the store closed. As he sat drumming his fingers on his desk, his telephone blurred. It was Rufus Bland's sidekick: Shard had not been contacted yet, but the military in Rinteln, when asked if by any chance he had been picked up by army transport at Hanover, confirmed that he had. They also reported that he had called in at BMH and had had an interview with Major Bruce, who had refused any further information. All this conveyed nothing at all to Hedge.

Shard, who already had the address of Wolfgang Brosak's laboratory from Gerda Schmidt, walked through lying snow from the hospital into Rinteln proper. It was a longish walk, over a bridge crossing the Weser and into the town centre. In the town centre, outside a grim-looking church, Shard enquired the way. Another ten minutes' walk brought him into a small industrial area of factories and store sheds, nothing spectacular.

Here he found Brosak's laboratory.

This, too, was fairly small-scale. There were barred windows and a heavy door. Shard peered in through the bars, saw two or three men working at benches, clad in dirty white overalls. Other men and a woman moved about. The place was brightly lit; the day was dull with the snow, which had begun to fall again. Shard went to the door, found a bell-push. His ring was answered after a short wait. One of the white-overalled men came to the door.

'Yes?' the man asked.

'Herr Brosak?'

'Herr Brosak sees people by appointment only. You have such an appointment, Herr—?'

'Harris,' Shard said smoothly. 'No, I've no appointment. But I had business at the British military hospital, and I've been referred on to Herr Brosak. I understand he has been helpful to the British doctors.'

'*Ja.* Your business?'

Shard waved a bunch of papers given him by Major Bruce, the bumph from the Ministry as he'd called it. 'I'm from London. The Department of Health.' He went into his spiel; Herr Brosak, he said, was regarded as an authority on rats. He would appreciate his help if he could spare the time.

'Wait,' the German said.

The heavy door was shut in Shard's face. He waited, huddling into the upturned collar of his thick anorak against the falling snow. It was bitterly cold now, the snow driven by an icy wind that was causing heavy drifting. After some five minutes the man came back. Herr Harris could enter; Herr Brosak had consented to see him but could not spare much time. 'Come,' the man said. He stepped back, holding the door open. Shard stepped into welcome warmth. Inside the doorway there was a hardboard partition that shut the working section of the laboratory off from view. He was led along a passage and up a steep flight of narrow stairs at the end. There was a curious smell on the air, light but pervasive. And unpleasant. Shard was unable to identify it. Another passage led from the head of the stairway,

118

with a number of doors on either side. The guide stopped at one, and knocked. A harsh voice responded, and the man opened the door.

Shard went in.

A short, thickset man was seated at a desk smoking a very large cigar. A box on the desk indicated that the cigar was named Adenauer after an earlier *Bundeskauzler* of the German Federal Republic. The man half rose, then subsided again. He waved the cigar towards a chair at the left of his desk.

'Sit, Herr Harris.' He spoke in English. 'Kindly state your business quickly. I am busy, you will understand?'

'Of course, Herr Brosak. I am sorry to bother you—'

He was cut short by a coarse, unpleasant laugh. 'Always you British seek my advice—me, a German. Oh, I am flattered, yes, I am flattered! But it is to a German hospital that I would prefer to be called for my assistance. And now London comes to me for my help! Well, Herr Harris, what do you wish to know?'

Shard, who on sitting down had noted that the white-overalled man had remained inside the room, spoke of rats and the problems they were causing in Great Britain. He had, he said, spoken to Major Bruce at the hospital about this.

'Major Bruce, yes. The hydrophobia man.'

'I understand you were of great help to him.'

'That is so, Herr Harris.'

Shard said, 'It's occurred to me that there may be some connection between this hydrophobia and rats.'

'You asked this of Major Bruce?'

'No, I didn't, Herr Brosak. It occurred to me only after—'

'What, precisely, has occurred to you?'

'That a proliferation in the rat population in Britain could assist the spread of rabies perhaps.'

'But there is no rabies in your country.'

'No,' Shard agreed, 'but we're concerned about the opening of frontiers, easier access, and the suggested abandonment of many of the quarantine laws, under the EEC—'

'Because of the rats?'

'Not just because of the rats, Herr Brosak, although if they're still a problem when the quarantine laws are done away with, then—'

'Yes, I understand, Herr Harris. I think you need not worry. Not, that is, about your rats. The whole of the British race, Herr Harris, is composed of rats.' Suddenly, like a striking snake, Brosak's right arm shot out almost horizontally. *'Heil Hitler,'* he said in a frenzied voice. From behind Shard, the salutation was repeated.

Suddenly, Shard felt a sense of danger, a cold feeling that all was not as it should be. He looked from one man to the other. The man in the white overall was standing stiffly at attention, almost as if on parade in the days of the Third Reich, staring over Brosak's head as though he were facing the physical presence of his long dead Führer. Or perhaps he saw Brosak as his Führer now. A moment later there was a nod from Brosak and the man by the door brought his hand sharply down and across his body. A revolver came out and was held steadily aimed at Shard's head.

Brosak gave his harsh laugh again. 'Not Herr Harris, I think, but Herr Detective Shard from London.' Rising to his feet he gave an ironic bow towards Shard. 'I am most gratified that you have delivered yourself into my hands.

Bloodlessly—though that is something that will not long endure, Herr Shard. I think you have been too trusting, like so many of the stupid British.'

Shard gave himself a shake mentally. He had been caught right off guard by Brosak's sudden change of tune. It was quite inconceivable, of course, that Major Bruce should be in any way involved, likewise Trudi Palmer.

'Gerda Schmidt,' he said bitterly.

'Yes, Gerda Schmidt, a loyal Nazi.'

Brosak went on to say that Gerda Schmidt's part was not played out. More than this, he refused to say. But he indicated that there were matters on which he wished to be fully informed and that the vehicle for this information would be Herr Shard. The Party, he said, had always been very expert in extracting information. Those who had lived under Herr Hitler and Dr Goebbels had lost none of their touch.

Hedge had made some enquiries and had established that Father Christmas packed up and went home by way of a beer cellar at 5.30 each day except Saturdays when he remained on duty for the benefit of the children of working parents until 8.00 p.m.

Today was Saturday.

A long time to wait. Hedge didn't like waiting. At a little after four o'clock he went along to the stores and lurked in the vicinity of Father Christmas's grotto as the children, happy, anticipatory or just plain fearful, queued and went in. He heard the vociferous Germanic complaints when the undesired present was handed over by Father Christmas. This he heard from round the other side by the grotto exit, where he remained, as he hoped, unseen by Father Christmas himself.

He was not unseen by other persons. He was observed by a keen-eyed female assistant in the leather goods sector of the store, situated not far from the grotto's exit; and this good woman hastened to make a report to her departmental chief.

'An old man, lurking, Herr Forster.'

'Ah. For shoplifting, Frau Spellman.'

'No, I do not think so, Herr Forster.' She lowered her voice, looked around carefully, about to speak of things that were better not said too loudly. 'The Father Christmas,' she said obliquely in Herr Forster's ear.

123

'The Father Christmas, Frau Spellman?'

'The *little children*, Herr Forster! The old man is regarding them as they emerge from the Father Christmas.' Frau Spellman's tone was heavy with accusation; a very full bosom heaved with indignation. 'Such people!'

'I shall look for myself, Frau Spellman.'

The departmental manager moved across the floor towards the exit from the grotto. He came up behind Hedge, who was staring at the children as they came through, having nothing better to do for the time being.

'Your pardon, *mein herr.*'

Hedge started, giving quite a jump. He turned. 'Yes, what is it?'

'Ah. You are English.'

'Yes, of course I am. Who are you, if I may ask?'

Forster identified his function in the store. 'Perhaps you have a grandchild, visiting Father Christmas?'

'No, I haven't,' Hedge answered irritably.

'No child at all?'

'No.' Hedge began to see the way the wind was blowing; he had not forgotten the vile accusation of the NATO supremo's son that same morning. He reddened.

He said, 'I don't know why I'm being subjected to a kind of—of interrogation. I'm here to observe you Germans in your natural habitat. You're of interest to us British. Especially at Christmas time, don't you know?'

'No, I do not know. I am told you have been here for quite some time. This is not welcome, for the good name of the store. I must ask you to leave immediately, *mein herr.*'

'I most certainly shall not,' Hedge snapped, his colour rising further. 'I have every right to be here, and I—'

The departmental manager cut him short. Stiffly he said, 'I have made my request. If you do not do as I ask, you will be removed forcibly from the store, and the police will be called.'

Hedge was furious, both at the imputation against his character and at the wretched German's act in baulking him of his mission. He was about to give the man a piece of his mind when he became aware of something going on behind him. He turned round. Father Christmas's rear view could be seen departing, moving away through the store, yet the emergence of the children was continuing unabated. Hedge ticked over: Father Christmas alias Logan had been relieved by another man. Perhaps that happened only on Saturdays, the late-opening day. Or perhaps it occurred every day, and at specified intervals. In which case he now had no idea at all which Father Christmas was Logan. In the meantime the departmental chief was waiting and was become impatient. Hedge glowered, knew he was beaten on all counts. 'Oh, God damn and blast all you foreigners! None of you has any savvy at all.'

He swung savagely and bounced away through the store, in the wake of Father Christmas, the one who just might be his quarry. He saw the red-clad figure vanish through what seemed to be a staff doorway. He really had no idea what to do now. He dithered, then made up his mind. There would be a staff exit somewhere on the ground floor, or perhaps from the basement. He would find it. He trundled down the stairs, glad enough to put room between himself and the wretched shopman. He was totally unaware that a young woman who had been examining handbags in the leather section was following at a discreet distance behind him.

He emerged into the street, into the snow and the wind. Shivering and very angry he pulled up the collar of his dark blue greatcoat and sunk his face down into it. Moving around outside the store, he identified what he believed was the staff exit. He waited, keeping the exit in view as he perambulated up and down to keep his circulation going. He pondered on Shard; this sort of thing was Shard's job, and Shard should have been here in West Berlin to do it. He wondered what Shard was up to; wasting his time probably. Policemen were very inclined to do just that. They had routine minds, were unable to see the wood for the trees. Basically, their minds were untrained.

He hadn't long to wait.

One or two persons, store workers possibly on shifts like Father Christmas, began to emerge. After some half-dozen had come out, Hedge believed he had pinpointed Logan. A man of similar build to the Father Christmas he had moved past with the American boy, now without the beard. It was true he didn't look, facially, like the Logan Hedge remembered, but so very many years had passed and very old persons, Hedge had found, tended to look alike, like Chinamen, all similarly pinched and grey with their geriatricity.

Then came the clincher.

The man hailed a taxi. The voice, again, was Logan's. Hedge was convinced of that. And a taxi! Father Christmases, genuine ones, didn't take taxis to and from their work, they were poor people, scraping the bottom of the financial barrel in order to get together some cash for their Christmas cheer. Which made the whole thing even more alarming. As that fellow Rufus Bland had said, Logan could hardly be a poor man. He had made his millions in the past and he could scarcely have got through the lot. Obviously, he had some nefarious reason for what he was doing. Hedge hailed another taxi and told the driver to follow the first one. Behind Hedge, the young woman acted in similar fashion. The convoy moved off into the traffic flow. Hedge, sitting on the edge of his seat and peering anxiously ahead past his driver, wondered what Logan's purpose could possibly be. Then he remembered, once again, his own morning sojourn with the son of the General Officer Commanding the NATO forces, an important man. Within the alliance a *very* important man indeed. More kidnap, more pressure to further Logan's mad schemes? Well, it was possible, even though that boy had turned up quite fortuitously without his mother. Logan could have been spying out the lie of the land, as it were, guessing that a small boy would be only too likely to be taken to see Father Christmas. Assessing the possibilities, that sort of thing. And, of course, there were other important persons, British and American, in West Berlin and some of them had children with them, all probably kidnappable. Rufus Bland was one; there would be others in the Consulate-General.

Really, it was quite a thought. If he, Hedge, could bowl out some nastiness of that sort, it would be a fine feather in his cap. Naturally, he wouldn't be going into action on his own, unsupported; that wasn't his job. But if he could, as it were, lead the way to a capture...well, that was just as good. Once he knew where Logan was living, once he could establish the man's identity beyond a doubt, then he would see to it that Shard was brought back posthaste to where the action was.

And that would be when he would have his heart-to-heart talk with Shard, make him see that it was in the national interest for Logan to be—well—*silenced,* somehow. Hedge shivered again when he thought about his London kidnappers. But now it simply had to be a case of first things first.

7

Shard's interrogation was not to take place in Brosak's laboratory, which Shard believed was probably the source, or one of the sources maybe, of the rabies vaccine production, the filth that was to be let loose, on Logan's word, against the West.

He was held in a small room in the laboratory building until after nightfall, his ankles and wrists tied and the door heavily bolted. There was a small window, uncurtained and set high in the wall; through this Shard could watch the fading daylight and make some assessment of the time, though his reckoning was thrown out to a large extent by the snowfall and the resulting overcast. But by his guess it was after 4.00 p.m when two men came for him, two men armed with Kalashnikov automatic rifles, and his ankles though not his wrists were untied.

He was taken along a passage that opened into the back part of the premises, a fair-sized yard with sheds and store-houses and three lock-up garages. By now the fall of snow had stopped, but there was a depth of some three feet piled around the cleared yard and when a car, a big Citroën, was backed out from one of the garages Shard saw that the tyres had been fitted with chains.

The rear near-side door was pulled open. 'In,' one of the men ordered, prodding his Kalashnikov into Shard's back. He got in. The other man got in beside him. In front, the driver sat alone. The Citroën was driven away at once. Shard, with his hands tied behind his back, was uncomfortable. The drive was a long one. After what seemed like a couple of hours the car was stopped near what was perhaps an all night café, anyway a place of refreshment. The driver got out and came back with four paper mugs of coffee and some sandwiches. All this time, none of the men spoke. When Shard asked questions he was told to save his breath. But, as the drive continued and he picked up more road signs he believed he was being taken into East Germany.

And that could mean Logan, if the Magdeburg sighting had been genuine.

It began to look like a rival cutting-out operation. Why else should convinced Nazis be entering East Germany?

To Hedge's chagrin, his taxi driver had lost Father Christmas. Lost him utterly in some very unsalubrious area of West Berlin.

The taxi stopped. The driver said, 'I am sorry. But it is of no use continuing.'

'So I see,' Hedge said, furious. 'I don't consider you at all competent. A London taxi would—'

'London, yes. Oh, they are so brilliant in London. Like all things that are British.'

'I don't like your tone,' Hedge said angrily. 'There's no need for sarcasm, and I'd be—'

'If you do not like, you get out pronto,' the taxi man said, angry himself now. The Englishman's manner was highly patronising and haughty. 'But first, the fare.' He named a sum; in Hedge's view this was extortionate and he began to demur. For the second time that day he was threatened with the attentions of the police and he paid up. No tip. The taxi was driven away at a high and obviously contemptuous speed, the action of a maniac, Hedge considered. He

133

wished he was back in London. London might be filthy, litter everywhere and acres of chewing-gum trodden into the once pure pavements of Piccadilly, and foreigners all over the place, but at least it was still British and he knew his way around.

Here, he didn't. He was utterly lost.

He stared about him, suddenly very afraid. There were mean streets all around —he was near a cross-roads and he could see four ways at once. None of them beckoned. There were not many people about and such as there were appeared to be foreigners. Germans, of course. And the Germans, forgetting what had happened to them during the war, had become extraordinarily cocky. But of course so had the common people in London...

Not a subway in sight. Not a bus. But there was, as Hedge now saw, another taxi. This was stopped by the kerb fifty or so yards back along one of the four streets. From it, a girl was emerging; Hedge started towards the taxi, lifting his umbrella and waving it. Halfway along, he met the girl. A polite man, he lifted his bowler hat.

'Your taxi,' he said in semi-German.

'May I...you have finished with it, Fräulein?' Gerda Schmidt was a pretty girl; Hedge ogled her. For this evening, at all events, Logan was gone. And Hedge was suddenly lonely.

Gerda Schmidt smiled at him, looking demure. She said, 'I saw the argument.' She spoke in English, not very well, but Hedge appreciated the gesture for it meant she had immediately recognised him as an Englishman, a compliment of course. 'I think you are, what do you say, abandoned?'

'Lost certainly, Fräulein. These damned taxi drivers—so rude and unhelpful.'

'It is a habit of theirs, yes. Perhaps I can help?'

There was something in the girl's eyes, a sort of come-on look. Hedge was to realise later that he should have been warned. The girl was in her early twenties, he estimated; he was quite sadly over sixty. And she didn't look like a prostitute, such as would easily enough disregard age in favour of hard cash. She wasn't that sort at all. But she was undoubtedly seductive.

He said, 'Well—perhaps you can. It's really very kind of you. As I said, I'm utterly lost. If I might make use of your taxi? But perhaps you've told the driver to wait?' She might have some business down here, for all Hedge knew.

'I told you, I saw the argument and that is why I stopped. You may come with me in my taxi and I will drop you wherever it is you wish to be dropped.'

'That's extremely kind of you, young— Fräulein.'

Again she smiled, right into his eyes. 'It is no trouble. Come.' She turned away towards the taxi. Hedge followed, scarcely able to believe his good fortune. He walked by her side, all friendly. She wore a seductive perfume, an expensive one, he guessed. She wore a fur coat, possibly only nylon or something like that but it added to the atmosphere. Something sinful—yet still not a prostitute. Hedge began to preen; he knew that a large number of young women preferred older men, men of stature and attainment, men of experience and mature charm. So many of today's supposedly educated young men were effete, dirty, yuppy, dressed hideously and had no manners. They treated women like chattels, Hedge was sure...as they approached the taxi Gerda Schmidt asked what address she should give the driver.

Hedge risked it. He gave her a winning smile; the result was oily. 'Wherever you suggest, Fräulein,' he said, his voice somewhat hoarse now—hoarse and urgent. Having spoken, he feared, just for a moment, that he might have gone too far, been too forthcoming and obvious. But no; the girl returned the smile, took his arm, gave some address to the driver, one that Hedge didn't catch, and they got into the taxi. The driver turned his vehicle back the way it had come and inside the cab hands intertwined very satisfactorily. Hedge felt a devil.

Gerda Schmidt was on the telephone from her flat. She was calling a number in Magdeburg. She was very shaken up; there was blood on her face from a head wound, her clothing was torn and dishevelled, and there was a gash on her leg. She said, 'The big, fat codfish...he is gone. I am sorry. It was not my fault. I had him hooked, and then there was this accident. It happened not far from the checkpoint, in a side road. There was this lorry...such a very big smash, though except perhaps for Hedge no-one was very badly hurt, which is so surprising—'

'Then Hedge—'

'Hedge was following a Father Christmas —this I saw, but I do not know why he was interested in a Father Christmas. Now he is gone.'

The voice rattled angrily along the wire, demanding further details of Hedge, where he had gone and why?

'Listen, please,' Gerda Schmidt said wearily. 'At the accident scene was passing another lorry that did not stop for more than a moment. In the force of the impact, this Hedge was propelled through the door of the taxi that had flown open. Something caused him to lift...and he went over the tail board of the lorry as it drove slowly past, I could not—'

'Where now is this lorry, please, Gerda?'

'I do not know, how can I, I was hurt and upset. But on the side of the lorry was inscribed the name of a firm, which I do not remember, and this firm was in Dresden. I think that your Hedge is now somewhere in East Germany, perhaps making willy-nilly for Dresden.'

Shard's enforced drive had continued into the German Democratic Republic. There was no trouble at the frontier posts; *glasnost* ruled now, in any case. Neither, however, was there any opportunity for Shard to turn any tables. As a precaution, he was told, the barrel of the revolver was brought down hard on his head, twice. He dropped into unconsciousness. He didn't hear his captors explaining that he was a victim of paralysis going to his home in the Democratic Republic to see for the last time his old mother, who was dying. Faked-up papers were virtually brushed aside; *glasnost* again. The frontiers were free for all now, both ways.

The drive went on inside East Germany. When Shard came round his head ached abominably and he felt thirsty and sick. They drove through towns and he saw the vast difference that lay between the two Germanys even after the greater freedoms had been permitted, even after the fall of communism. Here was poverty, sad-looking women queueing outside shops that needed paint, shops that appeared to have little to sell. There were placards and posters demanding the reunification of East and West Germany, a concept for which, as Shard knew, there was a strong desire among the non-communist population in East Germany, and among a strong neo-Nazi resurgence. Mangy dogs roamed past the placards, lifting their legs, cats were chased across mean streets. The free economy, the capitalist economy, took time to develop. It was vastly depressing. It was not Shard's problem, however. He had others currently. The Citroën went on, taking it fast, through different kinds of terrain, mountains, rivers, flat agricultural country, industrial sites all smoke and grime where the factories were working at all, gloom and stagnation where they were not in production.

But even in those places there had been an attempt, probably a municipal one, to bring some sort of cheer by way of decoration. The flags and bunting, the holly, the tinsel, hung damply over the drifted snow. Father Christmas drove his sleigh, just like in London, over the portico of what looked like a Town Hall.

It was Christmas Eve now.

Sitting between his guards in the back of the car Shard thought about his home. He would be missed, and Beth would be worrying because he hadn't been in touch. She always did; it was a failing he couldn't cure her of. And Christmas was a rotten time to be missed, a trying time for a worrying wife. Mrs Micklem wouldn't be helping; she always sounded disapproving of Simon Shard and because of this contrived, possibly—just possibly—without intent, to make his absences sound suspicious. As though, without ever saying so precisely, Simon had some ulterior purpose. For instance, another woman. She had often reflected aloud that policemen could always find easy excuses; she reflected lightly and with a laugh but Shard knew that it hurt Beth badly. Once he'd had it out with her, telling her off good and proper, but, just like her, she'd managed to wrong-foot him by saying, archly, that if he had nothing to hide, then what was there to worry about?

With Mrs Micklem you couldn't win.

In the Foreign Office the reports were coming in, largely from Number Ten and the Home Office and Scotland Yard, the Yard co-ordinating the nationwide police searches for the rabies-infected compounds. If they existed. The one in Scotland had been cordoned off distantly but not yet investigated. Discussions were taking place between the Home Office, the Department of Health, the local police authority and persons representing the animal rights organisations. No-one appeared able to reach a decision. And something worse had happened: the press had got hold of the story. Without the full facts, such as they were known, to go on, they were busy writing fiction. At any moment rabies was to be let loose on the population. Various reasons were given as gospel truth: the government was being pressured to release a number of IRA prisoners in Northern Ireland and on the mainland; CND was using threats in order to have the nuclear submarines recalled from their patrols and immobilised and de-missiled; the disbandment of NATO was being demanded by Colonel Gaddafi from his Libyan stronghold. The ayatollahs and mullahs in Iran were demanding increased rights for Muslims in the British Isles. The Dublin government was responsible and the cats and dogs and bats and so on would be released on the word from the Irish President unless Northern Ireland was handed back lock, stock and barrel to the Republic.

All that and more.

The result had been panic. Everyone

was demanding action. Downing Street had been cordoned off but the mobs were out in Whitehall and Parliament Square. The political parties were in a dither. This had the makings of a national emergency, of course, and they should all be pulling together and they knew it; but the leaders had been for so long conditioned to making party political points that they didn't. The Conservatives wanted to intensify the search and destroy all possible animal life by any means practical, including flame-throwers. Labour, needing the support of the Greens and the animal rights protesters, blamed the Tories for years of Hefferite policies leading to a total lack of moral standards and no concern for the ordinary people (or the ordinary animal). The Greens, who hoped to net the animal rights vote at the next election, not so far off as it happened, wanted the affair handled with kid gloves and no cruelty. It was not the fault of the animals, after all. That should be recognised. At the same time, naturally, the people (also blameless) had to be protected. They advanced a weird theory that the threat was being backed by a consortium of wood barons in South America who had been infuriated by British attempts to stop them cutting down the rain forests. Non-politically, an influential group of scientists of Cambridge University said that the government had a duty to keep an eye on the ozone layer and the greenhouse effect if any kind of chemical action was considered against the rabid animals. If they were rabid.

In Downing Street this was greeted with anxious hilarity. But the Prime Minister, Christmas Eve or not, broadcast to the nation. There was *absolutely* no cause for alarm, Mrs Heffer said; the government had the situation under *very firm control*. Any hard news would be made public immediately it was advisable so to do, by way of BBC announcements on TV and radio, and in the press. The threat was being taken very seriously but the Prime Minister did not for one moment believe it would ever come about. Everyone was heartily wished a happy Christmas and adjured not to let any anxieties spoil the festive fun. Notwithstanding all this, the TUC decided to convene a special meeting as soon as possible after Christmas so that NUPE in connection with the AEU could demand that a strike be called, a general strike on matters of principle, the principle not at this stage being spelled out in full but hinted to be directed against the government for its negative handling of what might become a life-and-death matter for all trade unionists.

Next morning, while the faithful were at early Communion in churches throughout the land, a Scottish policeman was bitten by a dog with foam at its mouth, a dog that had somehow escaped from the remote compound in the Sutherland glen. During the following night the policeman began to show early signs of hydrophobia. The speed of advance seemed to indicate the Logan strain.

'That's done it,' the Foreign Office Under-Secretary of State said. He was on the telephone to Scotland Yard. 'What the devil do we do now?'

'That's the Home Secretary's problem,' the Commissioner of Metropolitan Police answered, not having the faintest idea of what could possibly be done until all departments concerned had made up their minds and agreement had been reached. 'Is there any word yet from Shard?'

'Not a thing. I'd hardly expect it yet. When an operator's in the field, you don't—'

'Yes, quite. Just an enquiry—'

'I've got Hedge out there too, now. In West Berlin.'

'Oh, my *God.*'

The Under-Secretary was defensive. 'We're very pushed, you know. And some back-up was needed. A co-ordinator on the spot.'

'Well—yes, I suppose so.' There was a pause. 'Anything further on that suicide? You know what I mean.'

'Yes, I do. And no there isn't. But the investigation is under way.'

'D'you think there's a connection, Under-Secretary?'

'That's what I'm having investigated. Working back, if you follow—back to Logan. I'd rather not commit myself further than that just now.'

The call was cut. The Under-Secretary leaned forward, his elbows on his desk, his face in his hands. He was dead tired and also at his wits' end. He himself believed in the threat. The world held so many weirdos these days, men—and women—capable of virtually anything, any

146

nastiness imaginable. Or even unimaginable, like the rabies. Thankfully, the rabies *per se* was not the business of the FO; but it seemed as though only the FO could avert the threat. Currently via Shard. And of course Hedge. While the Under-Secretary was savagely cursing his luck at having been landed in such a pickle at Christmas, his security line rang again.

The Consul-General in West Berlin.

Shard appeared to be out of communication. No-one knew what had happened or where he was, other than that he had last been reported at BMH Rinteln. Hedge had wanted him back in Berlin.

And now Hedge had vanished as well, no details known. Except for some ridiculous story about a Father Christmas.

In West Berlin there was a great to-do over Hedge. He had simply vanished, as it seemed, from the face of the earth. Of Gerda Schmidt there was no sign, nor was there any knowledge in official circles. Even the fact of Logan/Schreuder having had a grand-daughter had never been dug out by those moles whose job it was to probe. Father Christmas, however, was investigated and cleared.

147

And nothing came through about Shard. A security man was sent post-haste to the British Military Hospital in Rinteln and Major Bruce was interviewed. Apprised of the urgency Bruce spoke at last of Shard's interest in rabies and of his mission concerning rats to Wolfgang Brosak's laboratory in the town. This was immediately visited by the West German security people, backed by police, and was found to be deserted. There had been wholesale smashing of equipment, retorts and test-tubes and Bunsen burners plus a lot of gear that had the look of having been very sophisticated prior to smashing. Major Bruce, who had accompanied the investigation, advised that nothing be touched other than by medics clad in protective clothing. This he would arrange for and would make tests. Until then, no action.

The assumption was made, correctly, that Shard had been abducted, and could be anywhere. Word of this was sent in due course to Bonn and the Berlin Consulate-General, and to the Foreign Office in London. At the same time a warning was given to the brass of NATO. A rather vague warning, since no-one had any idea of what was really going on, much less how to combat it. But the documents mailed a few days later by Logan to the FO were again perused and more attention was paid to his demand that the West should go into military action against the Soviets while they were faced with so many internal problems.

The Cabinet, which was hastily called together, was in a quandary. Russia was now the good, happy friend of the West. But a minister remarked that the Soviet Union had once been friendly towards Adolf Hitler and his Third Reich. Mates together against Britain until Hitler had turned and attacked them. The inference being that you couldn't trust the Russians. There was another inference and this was that Logan might have a point. Iron Russia out once and for all and you really would have world peace for a long time to come.

This inference was not spoken, but its presence in the Cabinet room could be felt. To attack a country when it was in a sense down was a far better prospect than rabies.

It was noticed that there was a thoughtful frown on the Prime Minister's face. But the Prime Ministerial utterance was as ever firm and unequivocal, an utterance rooted in total certainty. No-one could ever give in to threats. Great Britain would not be coerced. Neither, of course, would the United States. There was a strong degree of impasse. The threat was still somewhat vague and its implementation was a matter of sheer conjecture. They must wait for further clarification, Mrs Heffer said, and this was greeted with relief. There was no need for anyone to make any decisions yet.

Hedge was feeling desperately ill.

His mind was confused as to what had happened to him. He recalled Father Christmas and a small boy, and a sort of shopwalker, an offensive man; he recalled a taxi ride and a young woman with expensive perfume and a fur coat. He recalled a lot of snow and a big bang followed by great pain happily of short duration—he recalled a curious feeling of flying through the air after which the pain had ceased very abruptly. Now it had returned in full measure. There was the stickiness of blood, there was a huge lump on his head which ached and throbbed most abominably, his right side felt as though it had been excavated by a can opener and he believed he had broken his left arm.

Also, he was rolling about willy-nilly on a moving wooden floor, one that heaved and cast him this way and that. He was very cold; the moving floor had no ceiling and a bitter wind was bringing in flurries of snow. There was the sound of a motor. Wuzzily, Hedge came to the conclusion that he was in a moving vehicle, empty but for himself and going he knew not where nor why.

He tried to crawl towards what he now realised was a tail-board. No use. The effort was far too great; he collapsed back into a bloodstained heap.

After a very long time, it seemed to Hedge, the vehicle stopped, coming to rest beneath the roof of some sort of garage, or perhaps a warehouse. Hedge lay and groaned. He heard men moving outside and after a moment one of them looked over the tail-board. There was an exclamation of astonishment, and some rapid gabble in German.

Hedge was asked to account for his presence.

He was in too much of a state to remember his German. He asked in a weak but hoarse voice where he was. He asked in English and this caused consternation. There was an interval during which no-one came to his assistance. He felt his very life's blood draining away fast. Then another man came, one who spoke English. Hedge asked again where he was.

'Dresden,' the new man said.

'Dresden. I am sick. I am very badly hurt. I believe I am going to die. The British Consul-General...'

'Yes?'

'In West Berlin...'

There was puzzlement in the air. 'West Berlin? Who are you?'

Hedge was babbling, feeling immensely ill. 'The Consul-General in West Berlin—'

'Dresden,' the man said, 'is in the German Democratic Republic.' He added, 'A city that you English *schweinhundts* obliterated with your bombs during the war.'

Men clambered aboard the lorry and Hedge was extracted, none too carefully. The telephones were used and Hedge was transported to hospital, unconscious again by this time. The police turned up soon after and a watch was mounted on the strange Englishman's sickbed.

Shard arrived in Magdeburg just after another nightfall; he had lost count of time but believed it now to be Christmas Day. In Magdeburg God was being accorded scant ceremony; the accent was on the temporal rather than the spiritual. There were sad-looking decorations similar to those Shard had seen in the other towns along the route. That was all. Driven through Magdeburg into semi-rural surroundings, the Citroën pulled into a wide gateway to draw up in the carriage sweep of an imposing private house.

All three men got out. Shard was ordered out as well. The West Germans had their guns handy but concealed beneath heavy great-coats. Shard was pushed towards some stone steps leading up to a massive front door. A bell was rung. They all waited. After some two minutes and another ring, the door was answered. It was answered by a tall man, elderly, a man who seemed to receive a shock at seeing the men, as though he had been expecting someone else.

153

'Herr Brosak,' he said. 'Why do you risk coming here?'

'Because other risks are greater,' Brosak said. All the guns were out now, menacingly. 'We have come for Schreuder. We know he is here. And we know you have attempted to double-cross us.'

The men pushed the tall man aside and went in with Shard. They went across a large hall and into a book-lined study with elegant leather armchairs and thick curtains. A table lamp was burning by a coal fire. The room was warm and comfortable. In one of the chairs by the fire sat an old man, white-haired and frail, and Shard knew he was now in the presence of Logan.

'Prime Minister's office.'

It was the Foreign Secretary himself on the line. 'Personal to the PM,' he said. 'This is urgent.'

'One moment, Foreign Secretary.' The voice was smoothly deferential. The Foreign Secretary held. The Prime Minister came to the telephone. 'Yes, Roly?'

'Hedge, Prime Minister.'

'Hedge?'

'My man Hedge—you'll recall—'

154

'Oh, yes, yes, I'm with you. He disappeared. Well?'

'He's been located. A set of unfortunate happenings, I gather—I haven't got the full story yet. But he's in hospital in Dresden.'

'*Dresden?*'

'Yes, Prime Minister. In the GDR.'

'I see. Well, Roly, he must be got out *immediately.*'

The Foreign Secretary gave an embarrassed cough. 'He's under police guard, Prime Minister—'

'Never mind that,' said Mrs Heffer crisply and energetically along the wire. 'I repeat, he *must* be got out. Through the *proper diplomatic channels,* of course—'

'I'm sorry, Prime Minister, but that won't be possible—'

'Not possible? Why not?'

'Because he's not supposed to be there, Prime Minister. There would be all manner of diplomatic fuss...we can't possibly own him now.'

8

The dog compound in Sutherland had proved a very astonishing false alarm. It was true that the unfortunate policeman had contracted rabies, but it was established that the biting dog, a Rottweiler, had not come from the compound. His owner had come forward; the dog had disappeared from his home in Inverness, making off on a prowl on his own, a hunting trip no doubt. The compound, when closed in upon by the police cordon, with veterinary surgeons and a man from the ministry, had turned out to be harmless. It was owned by an eccentric Scottish peer and his aged mother, a marchioness with a love of dogs, who had set up a reception centre in a remote area of their own estate. All the inmates had been strays rescued from the streets and possible death at the hands of sundry local councils all over the country and their dog wardens. The marchioness and her semi-lunatic son had been scathing about the anti-dog laws perpetrated a few years earlier. A scandal, they had called them, and they were doing their best to set right a wrong. Naturally enough, they had the animal rights people on their side and afterwards a great song and dance was made about the way the government was currently trying to turn people against man's best friend.

The extraordinary thing was that absolutely no sign was found, despite the intensity of the police searches everywhere, of any other compound, any assembly of dogs or cats whatsoever, always leaving aside the authorised pounds such as the Battersea Dogs Home and a number of refuges run by spinster ladies, largely in Sussex. These, and the dog and cat hotels scattered around the country for the reception of pets whose owners were on holiday, had all been contacted and cleared.

The total lack of success was remarked upon by the Home Secretary.

'I can only suggest a ruse of this man Logan's, Prime Minister.'

'How do you mean, a ruse?'

'A red herring, Prime Minister. He never had any such compounds at all.'

'Oh? Then how does he expect to spread this rabies?'

The Home Secretary shrugged. He had no idea, really. But he offered a suggestion. He said, 'It may not be dogs or cats at all. Anyway—not dogs. Cats are rather more ubiquitous and Logan may see no need for them to be kept in pounds. But there's the other aspect, one we've perhaps not considered sufficiently deeply, Prime Minister.' He paused weightily. 'Bats,' he said.

'Bats?'

'Yes. As you know, of course, Prime Minister, bats have been for some years a protected species. As a result they have proliferated. They're everywhere—in barns and lofts and—and other places where I understand bats congregate. They're a nuisance to farmers, to householders too in some cases. And there is the question of their—er—habits.' The Home Secretary coughed. 'Their urine. I'm told it contains the germs of rabies.'

'You mean if a bat pees on you, Walter, you might contract the disease?'

'I don't think there has to be an actual...I don't think the person has actually to be *urinated on*. There may be danger in the simple fact of the urine, the fact that bats do urinate and that the germs can be spread—'

The Prime Minister interrupted with a loud sigh. 'You may be right, I suppose. But I don't see what we can do about bats. They can't be controlled.'

'We could warn the clergy,' the Home Secretary said gloomily, 'but—'

'Why the *clergy*, for heaven's sake, Walter?'

'Belfries, Prime Minister. The bats live in church belfries as well as the other places I've mentioned.'

Mrs Heffer gave him a searching and sardonic look. Bats might spread disease if what the Home Secretary had said was true; but the theory didn't hold water. Not bats on their own. How was Logan, when he considered the time had come, to inform the bat population that they were to start urinating? A dog compound was a different matter; a sudden release of foaming mouths would certainly do the trick.

But there were apparently no compounds.

Impasse again. The Prime Minister, who had summoned certain ministers including the Home Secretary to Chequers, gave them a Christmas whisky and sent them packing. There were family matters to attend to now.

Logan had been a prisoner although there had been no special guard on him; physically he was too far gone to attempt an escape. Shard listened with interest to an exposition of what had happened in the last few days. It seemed that Logan/Schreuder the convinced Nazi had been cut out from the Federal Republic when word of his anti-Soviet plan had leaked, as most secrets do eventually in this age of moles and scant loyalty. The men who had nabbed him, the men now under Brosak's guns in this room, the men who had attempted a double-cross on Brosak, had been Nazis as convincedly as Brosak and Logan himself. But their loyalties had undergone a sudden change. They were now, as Brosak accused them, in the pay of the Soviets. To this they had no answer. They stood silent before the guns, their eyes moving this way and that, waiting their moment to try to turn the tables.

Shard felt remarkably superfluous. Why had he been brought here? Presumably, just because he'd turned up in the Rinteln laboratory at an awkward and inopportune moment. It would be more productive, perhaps, to turn his mind towards what Brosak intended to do with him. There had been that talk of an interrogation; that had not yet come. Another productive line would be to consider how he could best make a getaway before it did come.

Currently, that looked difficult.

Meanwhile, Brosak was interrogating the renegades.

And they were not answering.

Brosak wanted to know just how much had been revealed to the Soviet authorities. The response was a series of shrugs; they didn't know.

'I shall perhaps stir your memories,' Brosak said. He lifted his gun. It was a revolver and after producing it earlier he had fitted a silencer onto it. He now thumbed back the firing pin and held it ready cocked. 'You will speak quickly,' he said, 'or I shall smash the knee of you, Klaus.'

Klaus was identifiable to Shard by the sudden flicker in the eyes: Klaus was the tall man who had answered the door. He licked at his lips. He darted glances right and left but didn't speak. Didn't dare to, was Shard's estimate, because of what his mates might do to him if he did.

Brosak's voice was quietly threatening. 'Come now, Klaus. We have been good friends and comrades in the past. We share many good memories of the old days of the Reich. Even if your loyalties have changed, this does not erase the happy memories. I do not wish to destroy your knees, Klaus, to make you a cripple for the rest of your days. But be very sure that this I will do if you do not talk.'

Klaus licked again at his lips. There was a shake in his hands, Shard noticed. He probably knew that Brosak was a man of his word. But he said, 'We are all old now. There are not many years left. I did not wish to die with so much on my conscience.'

'The threat to peace,' Brosak stated. 'This is—'

'War in 1939 solved no problems. It made our situation desperate, and now that there has been peace for more than forty years things have so much improved. I decided I did not wish to destroy this.'

'Not even in the name of the Führer, Klaus?'

The atmosphere in the room was

extraordinary; Shard was aware, as he waited for Klaus to answer Brosak's question, of some emanation of an evil past, of a resurgence of days best left buried.

Klaus, trembling, said, 'The Führer is dead, Wolfgang. You cannot bring him back to life. Your schemes and Schreuder's, they can only end in failure. And in so many deaths.'

Brosak said, still quietly, 'So you decided to run, and take your treachery to Moscow.'

Klaus did not reply. He stood mute, shaking like a leaf, waiting for what was to happen.

Brosak said, his voice rising now, *'Heil Hitler!'* Then he squeezed the trigger of the silenced revolver. There was a muffled explosion, sudden contraction of the air, and a stench of gunsmoke, followed by a scream of agony from Klaus. The tall man fell like a suddenly cut-down tree, and blood spurted. Fragmented bones protruded from blasted flesh. The knee had turned into a red and gaping hole.

Brosak was unmoved. He re-cocked his revolver. The guns of the other men were ready also. Brosak said, 'Now who is going to tell me what I want to know?' He turned his head a little, towards the semi-derelict old man in the chair before the fire. 'You, Schreuder. *You* will not have changed your loyalties, I know.'

London was now in a kind of turmoil. There was simply no hard information, only the renewed use of frantic imagination by the press, or most of it. The experts had a field day once the festive season was declining into the usual extended holiday when the fortunate went to Switzerland for the ski-ing and the less affluent indulged in Do It Yourself around the home. Veterinary opinion was much in demand; everyone wanted to be able to diagnose rabies as soon as possible if the threat should materialise. So they mugged it up from the newspapers, knowing that with rabies any delay would probably be fatal. Rabies was discussed in pubs and works canteens and during office coffee breaks and in the homes throughout the land. The various newspaper articles were quoted, as were the opinions of the pundits on TV and the wireless. Terry Wogan had interviewed a vet, along with a representative of the Department of Health. Esther Rantzen had been after Whitehall's blood, and she had driven at once to Brighton to gather opinions in the streets. The general view was that, as usual, the government was not doing enough and that the lack of information, of action too, was nothing less than a scandal.

'A bloody disgrace,' a well-dressed woman emerging from the Grand Hotel said. Others said more or less the same thing. Everyone, by now, knew what to look out for: in the first place, of course, foaming dogs and erratically-behaving cats. Rats and mice were to be stood well clear of. Not many people were bothered about bats. Not in Brighton, anyway. Then the symptoms: after about six weeks to two months—in the case of the normal strain, this was, but the new strain would be very much shorter—after a therefore currently unknown interval from being bitten by almost anything, even another human with the disease upon him, there would be dullness, depression, irritability and a general malaise. (As Esther Rantzen remarked laughingly, everyone suffered from that from time to time, so what?) But very soon there would come a difficulty, slight at first but worsening, in swallowing. The throat would appear to contract; and the voice would become hoarse so that the sufferer would emit a sound like barking. There would be a rise in temperature, perhaps to 40 or 41 degrees. Thereafter the disease would escalate and the most violent and painful throat spasms would follow any attempt to swallow liquids so that the patient would dread the drinking of water. Also, the sufferer would become ultra-sensitive to any sound, any slightest variation such as from passing traffic or even footsteps in the sickroom. A draught of air, or the sound of splashing water, would produce horrifying convulsions. The afflicted person would soon become delirious and might try to bite anyone in the vicinity.

And the end?

'Death, generally,' the man from the Department of Health told Terry Wogan. 'From general exhaustion, or heart failure, or asphyxia from the throat spasms.'

'I see. And the recovery rate, John?'

The man from the Department shrugged. 'Very hard to be precise, Mr—Terry.' He was being evasive; he had no wish to spread alarm and despondency. When the interview was over, he told Terry

Wogan, privately, that in cases that had been diagnosed as rabies and which had subsequently recovered, it was believed that the original diagnosis had been wrong.

Which spoke for itself. Mr Wogan went home with uncomfortable inside knowledge in his head. Sometimes it was better not to ask too many questions...

There had been a number of telephone calls across the Atlantic, Number Ten to White House, person to person. The President was an anxious, but at the same time a highly doubtful person.

'Just don't want to get involved,' he said, 'in something that could turn out to be somebody's idea of a great, big joke.'

'That's *not* the way we're seeing it over here, George.'

'Why, no, I guess maybe not, Charlotte, but...look, *we*'ve had nothing over here from this guy Logan, or Schreuder. Just nothing at all, and—'

'Let's suppose you do, George. What then?'

'Well, that's something I can answer better when it happens. If it happens.'

'It's often better to have a contingency plan, don't you think?' Mrs Heffer was tart.

'Well, maybe. I'll be giving it thought, that I do promise. But it sounds very hairy to me, real lunatic. The guy has to be stark, staring mad, you know that?'

Mrs Heffer breathed hard. 'It's crossed our minds, yes. But George...suppose it's for real. Mad or not...it could come about. Now: if it does, *Where does the USA stand? Can you tell me that?*'

There was a pause; a long one. The President could almost be heard thinking, his inner wish that he had his Secretary of State standing by his side almost manifesting itself along the airy five thousand miles of satellite telephone communication. Then, cautiously, he spoke to Great Britain: 'I guess, you know, that requires consideration, Charlotte. You'll understand that. I guess what you're suggesting, it's kind of a war situation, you know? I call that wacky, Charlotte, considering the Reds are out anyway—look at what happened to Ceauşecu, look at Czechoslovakia.'

'In the former satellite countries, yes, of course I agree. *Not* entirely in the Soviet

168

Union itself...or if it is, George, then I fancy it could be more apparent than real. Don't you?'

There was a curious sound along the line. 'Well, I guess I can't really commit myself on that, Charlotte. I suggest you call me back, okay?'

In Downing Street Mrs Heffer bit off a sarcastic retort. Call him back—when it would possibly be too late! In today's world, things so often moved with the speed of light. Rabies itself had apparently been speeded up. Mrs Heffer put down the telephone with an angry gesture. George's head had been turned ever since that meeting at Malta with Gorbachev in 1989, to which she, Mrs Heffer, had not been invited. The Americans would be the same as in 1914 and 1939...but, as a thought, that would never do. It would sound as though war, in the Prime Ministerial mind, was becoming a real possibility, a real option. The British public would never take war again. Just the fact, if known, that the Prime Minister had war in mind even as an outside possibility, might lose the Party the next election.

Hedge was now beside himself. He was

sitting up in hospital feeling better, but the future loomed as bleak and black as any Siberian night. He was seeing Siberia as no mere figment of his imagination. The plain-clothes man who had replaced the uniformed policeman by his bedside spoke volumes. Figuratively, that was. In fact, he said nothing. Hedge wished fervently that the man would open his mouth and say something reassuring. All Hedge's questions had remained stonily unanswered.

He was in a tizzy.

Where, for God's sake, was Shard?

Shard should never have allowed him to get into this terrible predicament. What was the assistant under-secretary, or the Under-Secretary—and come to that the Secretary of State himself—doing about him?

Nothing, probably. Of course, they wouldn't know...and for his part he couldn't communicate. In the circumstances, the circumstances of his being despatched to West Berlin, he knew he couldn't reveal his status to the Communists. If he did, they would treat him as a spy.

On the other hand, they might not,

might they? He was a person of importance in the Foreign Office, after all. Persons of his rank didn't spy. Perhaps, from time to time, like now it might be said, they found things out. But that was different.

Hedge dithered, pulled the sheet and blanket closer to his chin, since the room—a side room it was, not a ward—was chilly. Then he pushed them down again; they were dirty, had probably been used by someone else since last they had been washed. They might contain the germs of some disease...

Rabies, the whole reason, really, for his current situation?

Hedge shook with horror and tried again to ask his urgent questions, concerned mainly with trying to establish what the wretched Communists meant to do with him. He wished he was at home, even without Mrs Millington, who, if in fact she was back from attending upon her sister-in-law, would be worrying dreadfully about him.

His question remained unanswered still. The plain-clothes man stolidly read a Communist newspaper and as stolidly picked his nose.

Then there was a commotion. Doctor's

rounds. Just like the West; a bouncy little man in a black jacket traipsed along with his retinue of other doctors, sisters, nurses, what looked like social workers in dark blue coats and skirts and man-like shirts with neckties. They all came into Hedge's room, filling the entire space and submerging the plain-clothes watchdog, who protested, uttering the first sound to be heard from him. A social worker smiled at the man vaguely but otherwise he was ignored. So was Hedge; the whole procession looked at him and shook their heads and gabbled away in German but Hedge was not spoken to and understood only a word or two here and there. Of course, all foreigners always spoke very fast and were quite impossible to comprehend even if you did happen to speak their ridiculous lingo.

Having looked and gabbled they all went away again. Hedge became terribly agitated and began calling out, asking in a high voice for someone to come and help him. He rose from his bed and put a foot on the floor. The plain-clothes man got up immediately and pushed him back with very strong arms and then yelled out for a nurse who came and gave Hedge a sedative, injecting fluid into his buttocks with a needle.

The Dresden police had contacted their Foreign Affairs ministry.

'A man, an Englishman. Portly in shape. Upon him there are papers of the British Foreign Office. His name appears to be Hedge.'

'And entered, did you say, in the back of a lorry from the Western sector?'

'Yes—'

'What was in this lorry, what was it carrying?'

'The lorry was empty. It belongs to a farming co-operative producing largely sugar beet, with warehouse premises in the city.'

'Yes. I see. This Hedge. The British Foreign Office—he is perhaps of some importance, though why a sugar-beet lorry I really do not know. But the British are so curious. And he was injured? You must question the members of the farming co-operative, and the driver himself. Then report again.'

'Yes. And the man himself?'

There was a pause; then, 'I believe this to be a matter for Moscow. We have still our treaty obligations even though...and we must not tread too hard on the toes of Moscow.' There was still the fact of the Warsaw Pact—still in existence and never mind all that had happened in the last two or three years. East Germany, Wall or no Wall, Iron Curtain or no Iron Curtain, was more or less in the Soviet area of influence. 'The man is to be closely held until the affair of his curious entry is resolved.'

Later that day, when the effects of the sedative had worn off, Hedge, covered with bandages and plaster, was removed to the mind-bending confines of a police cell.

To Hedge, the cell had all the appearance of a torture chamber. There were heavy ring-bolts set into the walls, there was a raised plank for a bed, there were traces of blood, he believed, on the stone floor, there was no window but a glaring, unshaded electric light bulb stared down at him balefully from behind a sort of steel-mesh safety cover.

There was a grille, covered from the other side, in the immensely thick door. Hedge shouted through this, desperately. He needed to relieve himself, all the worry and uncertainty having, it seemed to him, to have congregated in his bladder.

A man came and the grille was uncovered. Hedge managed to make himself understood. The warder or whatever he was had some English.

'Piss, yes. Under the bed look.' The grille was shut again. Beneath the plank, Hedge found a chamber pot.

In the house in Magdeburg, Logan/ Schreuder had affirmed that indeed his loyalties had not changed. In rambling fashion he told Brosak how he had come to be where he was. 'Wicked men,' he said, coughing violently, almost a kind of spasm. When this had passed he went on, 'Men whom we trusted, you and I—all of us trusted them implicity to bring back the ideals of our beloved Führer.'

'Yes,' Brosak said impatiently. 'But now we have to—' He broke off. Schreuder had turned a nasty colour very suddenly, a greenish tinge coming over his features while his lips remained red, though quite quickly thereafter a bluish tinge appeared. The old man's breathing became laboured. Brosak started forward towards the fireplace. As he did so, the old man lurched sideways. Brosak caught him as he fell from his chair; Logan was a good deal heavier than he had appeared, and Brosak was taken off his guard when one of Logan/Schreuder's captors made a sudden move. There was a shout of alarm from one of Brosak's men as a heavily sprung cosh came down, just missing his head but striking his shoulder. Brosak, literally wrong-footed, staggered under Logan's weight, lurching towards the fire.

Logan fell into the glowing coals and flickering flames. Brosak, yelling imprecations, dragged the old man clear. With him came a number of glowing coals to drop upon the carpet and roll beneath the chair in which Logan had been sitting. At once a general mêlée started up, and shots were fired. A miniature battle took place around Shard, whose wrists were still tied. Within a matter of seconds the fire had taken hold and Logan's chair was ablaze. A trail of fire ran across the carpet towards the thick fabric of the curtains over the windows.

Shard moved, dangerously, between the legs of the men. He found a glowing coal, turned his back to it and set his teeth as, sitting on the carpet, he manoeuvred his tied wrists onto the red-hot coal.

9

Hedge, whose wristwatch had been removed along with his braces, and his shoelaces and his tie, had no idea how long he had been left in his dreadful cell, which smelled of urine. The chamber pot had not been emptied before he made use of it. The place was just like what he understood the Lubyanka prison in Moscow was like, bestial and harsh. Soon, no doubt, he would be removed to somewhere else and there would be an interrogation. But they appeared to be in no hurry, so far as he could tell. Not that he was able even to distinguish night from day; no daylight penetrated from anywhere at all. Meals were brought; nasty dry black bread, some tepid lentil soup, a jug of water. Not at all what he was used to; he thought again about Mrs Millington and about her cooking. Sadly, he had never really appreciated her.

Would he ever see her again?

Would they ever come for him so that

he could attempt to explain?

At last, they did.

The heavy door was jangled open. Two men stood there, hard-looking men, one of them carrying a Kalashnikov rifle, the other holding a large bunch of keys.

'Come,' the key-holder said. As Hedge obeyed and went through the door into a passageway, the man gave him a heavy shove. Hedge squealed with fright and surprise. It was undignified to be shoved like that, and the fact that he could do nothing about it robbed him of such self-confidence as he had left. He moved in obedience to the shove towards the end of the passage where there was a staircase, a stone-stepped one. He looked round questioningly, and the man with the rifle said something in German and nodded, so Hedge went up the stairs.

He was halted outside a door. The door was knocked upon and prisoner and escort were admitted.

At a desk set in front of a window, a thin man sat writing. This man, whose face was long and lined and sallow and somehow devilish, wore uniform, a curious and slovenly uniform, not smart like the communists of old would have been.

He didn't look up at Hedge's entry; he continued writing, filling in some sort of official form, Hedge saw. Hedge stood before him, tieless, no shoe-laces, no braces. His stomach was large, the waist-band of his trousers, made in Savile Row, was larger. He felt like a naughty schoolboy up before the headmaster.

It was, he believed, a good five minutes before the uniformed man spoke, and when he did speak it was brief and in English and uttered while still writing on his form.

'You are called Hedge.'

'I beg your pardon?' Did he, or did he not, admit anything at all? He'd thought about this in his cell and decided to play it by ear. But, faced with a decision now, he dithered.

'You are called Hedge. Kindly listen, Hedge, when I address you.' Hedge took a deep breath. Well, of course they knew; they had taken his wallet along with all the rest and he could scarcely hope to bluff his way out of *that*. He said, 'Yes.' It was probably all right; in the last war, if captured by the enemy, you could gave your name, rank and number.

'Of the British Foreign Office.'

'Well...yes, I am.' Actually, they might treat him better now, although, obviously, they had known it all along—his wallet again—his confirmation would mean they knew he knew they knew... Hedge gave it up and hoped for the best. He drew himself up a little, tried to look his rank. His trousers sagged a little further and he reached down to pull them up.

'You will keep your hands still, at your sides.'

'Yes...I'm sorry.'

At this point the man looked up, keenly, cold greenish eyes seeming to bore right into Hedge. 'Of the British Foreign Office. Why did you enter the Democratic Republic in the back of a sugar-beet lorry?'

Hedge said at once and with truth, 'I didn't know it was a sugar-beet lorry.'

The man snorted. 'You evade the question with stupid utterances, Hedge. Now answer.' He leaned forward across his desk and jabbed his ballpoint towards his victim. 'Why did you enter clandestinely from West Berlin?'

Hedge floundered. Father Christmas would be an unlikely story and in any case he must not speak about Logan whatever else he might be forced into saying. He said at last, 'It was involuntary, I'm afraid.'

'Not of your own volition?'

'Oh, by no means. I was, I think though I'm not sure, thrown in.'

'Thrown?' Scepticism abounded. 'By a person?'

'No, I doubt that. I really don't known...there was an accident and I was injured—I may have been *projected* in. I've been thinking about that,' he added. 'I—'

'That you come from the hospital with injuries we know, of course. That is genuine.'

'*I* am genuine,' Hedge said.

'And certainly there appears to have been an accident.'

'Yes indeed,' Hedge said, feeling happier.

'But we do not know what sort of an accident. The sugar-beet lorry has been examined and is not damaged.'

'The driver would—'

'The driver left his employment on his return from Berlin. He will of course be apprehended. Until he is, we are uncertain about you, Hedge. The driver made no report of an accident. Why not?' There was a shrug. 'We do not yet know. It was perhaps because the driver did not wish for involvement. Or perhaps it was because there was no accident to the sugar-beet lorry. That, we shall see.'

'When?' Hedge's heart was beating fast now. Damn and blast the lorry driver—why couldn't he have made matters clear upon his arrival? Hedge fumed inwardly. 'When?' he asked again, beseechingly.

'In due course.' The man filled in some more of his form. 'We believe it is possible you have entered the Democratic Republic clandestinely for certain reasons.'

'What reasons?'

The man shrugged again. 'Espionage, perhaps?' The cold eyes scanned Hedge's face, full of accusation. 'The age of espionage is not yet past. *Glasnost* has not altered some aspects of our lives.'

'I am not a spy.'

'We shall see—'

'I am a gentleman. Gentlemen don't spy. Certainly not when they're employed by the Foreign Office—'

The man stopped him with a lift of his ballpoint. 'I have said, we shall see, and that is what we shall do. This will in the meantime be referred to Moscow, with whom we still have the diplomatic links.

Also, depending on what is said to us by Moscow, by the Kremlin and the KGB, it will perhaps be referred to the British Foreign Office.'

'If you—'

'That is all. You will say no more.' Hedge wanted to say, for God's sake contact the FO immediately and they'll put me in the clear. But he was given no chance; at a signal from the uniformed man the guards seized him and he was taken from the room back to his cell.

The report was made to Moscow, on one of the thin man's forms which was at once telexed to the Kremlin. A pompous man, the report said, perhaps of little consequence but naturally no stone would be left unturned. The story of the accident was fishy. The man insisted he was not a spy. He was, he had said—and this had been particularly noted—a gentleman. There was also a little explanation; the term "gentleman" might be unfamiliar, in the sense the uniformed man understood Hedge to have used it, to the Russian mind. In the Soviet Union there were no gentlemen. It would not be a cogent reason not to be a spy. After Moscow had spoken,

Hedge would be interrogated again. And then another report would be made.

'They positively have Hedge, Foreign Secretary.' This was the Under-Secretary of State reporting by telephone.

'They?'

'The East Germans, Foreign Secretary, in Dresden. An unfortunate series of events, I gather—'

'They've communicated?'

'Moscow has, Foreign Secretary.' The Under-Secretary of State listened then spoke again. 'No, he's still in Dresden. So far as we know, that is. He's being held on a charge of illegal entry, via a sugar-beet lorry from West Berlin. Yes, Foreign Secretary, sugar-beet. In the back. Moscow is asking for clarification of his position. Asking, really, for us to claim him, I think—'

'And if we claim him—what then?'

'It's hard to say, Foreign Secretary. They've not actually said he would be handed back.'

'The buggers are never very forthcoming, are they?'

This was rhetorical; the Under-Secretary waited for more. The Foreign Secretary went on, 'We hold our horses, Roger. At this stage, we make no admissions. And give no information. The whole thing's too fraught in regard to Logan and this wretched scare, the rabies.'

'And Hedge, Foreign Secretary?'

'Must be left, I'm afraid. For now, anyway.'

'Yes, Foreign Secretary. Er...what reply shall I make to Moscow?'

'Oh, I'm sure you'll cope, Roger. Dream something up, something innocuous. You know the form.' The Foreign Secretary cut the call quickly before he could be pressured. It was Roger's job to handle delicate situations, return some smooth and non-committal reply to keep Moscow happy. The gist of it would be, of course, that nothing was known of anybody called Hedge in the Foreign Office. This, too, had its complications, because it was the job of the KGB to know all about highly-placed persons in the British Foreign Office and they were unlikely to fall down on their job. But the Kremlin would understand; diplomats the world over had their shorthand, and what they read into it wasn't really very important just so long as nobody made any actual admissions.

Once again there was a high-level discussion on rabies and the threat posed by Logan. *Said* to be posed by Logan; a good deal of scepticism was in the air even though Logan's documentation had been precise. There had still been no reports of any dog compounds being found; and cats still roamed the streets and delved into dustbins in alleys. Bats still flew from barns and belfries and lofts. An elderly woman alone in a big, old-fashioned farmhouse in Wensleydale in North Yorkshire had woken during the night and had heard a sound as though there had been a break-in. A courageous Yorkshire woman, she had put a dressing-gown over her nightdress and gone downstairs with a pitchfork which she customarily kept beside her bed. She had found all doors and windows secure but had seen a shadow flit across her back yard from a barn and this she had assumed to be an intruder. She had gone outside and called out but had received no answer and a moment later the legs of a bat had entangled themselves in her hair. This had unnerved her and she had run screaming to her car and had driven, bat and all, to her doctor. She had read the scare stories in the press and she feared rabies. The doctor had calmed her but in the circumstances had felt the incident worth repeating both to the police and the local Environment Health Officer and it was now likely to hit the press; thus it had been reported to the Minister for Health via Scotland Yard.

Mrs Heffer cast it aside. 'Just one old woman.'

'But it all adds fuel to the flames, Prime Minister.'

'Well, yes, I take your point. But there's nothing we can do about it, is there?'

There was not. Somebody remarked that it was all a storm in a teacup. No compounds found and there never would be. Logan was attempting to throw a scare.

'But why?'

'We just don't know, Prime Minister.'

'Logan, by all accounts—the files, you know—isn't the sort of man to make *jokes*, sick or otherwise. It does occur to me that the rabies business could be a *blind*, something to divert the nation's attention, if you follow.'

'Divert it from what, Prime Minister?'

Mrs Heffer shrugged. '*I* don't know, how should I? Let's say...something worse?'

The members of the Cabinet considered this with varying and mixed degrees of alarm and cynicism. The Defence Secretary murmured something about mustering all their resources as fast as possible and calling out the Territorial Army, by Royal Proclamation of a state of emergency. We had, he insisted when he got a hearing, to be ready. While the argument over this gathered strength the security telephone burred. It was the Foreign Secretary, Rowland Mayes, apologetic for his non-attendance. There had, he said, been word of Hedge. Making his report brief, he indicated what he had told the Under-Secretary of State.

The Prime Minister nodded into the mouthpiece. 'Yes, very wise. I concur, Roly.'

In Rinteln, Logan's laboratory had been ransacked for clues as to what had happened to Detective Chief Superintendent Shard. Nothing helpful had been found. Major Bruce and his paramedics had made their promised investigation into the research carried out by Logan and his team. In this, Bruce had been assisted by a veterinary officer from the British Army depot at Minden, not far from Rinteln. There was evidence that Logan, as Bruce had already known, had been working on hydrophobia in an attempt to find a more effective vaccine for its cure. Bruce made a report to BAOR HQ which was passed on to Bonn and the Ministry of Defence. The report lent no credence to any large-scale threat by Logan, whose research had been, apparently, on a small basis only. When this report, once in the hands of Whitehall, was leaked as usual, the press had another field day. They castigated the government for scaremongering and gave it as their opinion that everybody should as of now sleep soundly in their beds. There was a hint that the scare was not, perhaps, unconnected with Party politics, what with the election in prospect. In some way, as yet, unspecified.

The fire in the Magdeburg house had spread very fast indeed. Shard, once his wrists were free, had grabbed a Kalashnikov rifle from one of Brosak's men who had been overcome by fumes. There was a rush for the door. Shard, a handkerchief clamped over mouth and nose, made a dive for Logan, who looked in a very bad way by this time and was suffering from burns. Moving fast, Shard got a grip and dragged the old man through the door only just before the ceiling of the room came down in a heavy shower of plaster and dust and general debris that fell into the flames and fed them. Intense heat swept through behind Shard, shearing him and his burden.

Smoke began to fill the hall. From its cover, a couple of gunshots came. A bullet zipped past Shard's head, smacked into the woodwork behind him. He brought up the Kalashnikov and squeezed the trigger, firing blind into and through the smoke. There was a scream of pain, then feet running away fast, and no more gunfire.

Shard half carried Logan through the hall, feeling his way blindly through the smoke. He found the door; he carried Logan down the stone steps into breathable air. Brosak's car had gone, as had Brosak himself. While pushing through the smoke-filled hall, Shard had stumbled over a body. Flames were now coming out from the front door; the house was doomed. Shard had no idea how many of the men, on both sides, had died.

The first thing to do was to get away with

Logan before Brosak returned: he wouldn't be very far away and had no doubt decided to vanish for a while, just a while; soon now the police would be around, and a fire engine. The same considerations applied to Shard. With Logan, and with no pursuit currently, he went fast around the back of the house. Already people disturbed from their sleep were gathering in the front, in the roadway.

At the back of the house were fields. There was also Brosak, maybe some of his henchmen as well: from behind a hedge gunfire came. Brosak was taking the risk of being heard. Shard dragged Logan down to the ground and flattened beside him. There was no further gunfire. Then a few minutes later, as police and fire service sirens sounded in the rear, Shard saw the shadowy forms coming across from the hedge. There was no moon and the shadows were hard to pick up after the first glimpse. But Shard felt their approaching presence.

He waited, hoping that Logan wasn't going to die on him.

10

There was another conference, this time in the Soviet Foreign Ministry. The conference was to do with the illegal entry by sugar-beet lorry of Hedge into the German Democratic Republic.

'This Hedge.'

'Yes.'

'He is of course known to us, Comrade Foreign Minister.' The speaker, a senior Party member highly placed in the Soviet Foreign Service hierarchy, frowned in thought. 'It is very strange in my opinion.'

'Why is that?'

'Because of this Hedge. He is an important person in the British Foreign Office. Not a person who would normally be infiltrated. This makes me suspicious that the British have a very particular purpose in employing him—'

'As a spy, Comrade?'

There was a nod. 'Just so. A spy. This, of course, he denies according to the Germans. This is natural. Also, there has been a reply to our enquiry—the British have no knowledge of Hedge.'

'What does that mean, do you think, Comrade?'

'That the British are lying.'

'Yes, of course.' The Foreign Minister drummed his fingers on his desk. 'Why do you suppose they are lying, Comrade?'

The official shrugged. 'A normal ploy, Comrade Foreign Minister. But this time, more behind it, than meets the eye.' He paused weightily. 'You will, of course, remember what has appeared in the British press. Some threat of the spread of rabies. And the re-emergence from the dead of the man Logan, or Schreuder, the Nazi, now held in East Germany.'

'In Magdeburg.'

'Yes, Comrade Foreign Minister. Logan is to be brought to Moscow today for questioning. As you know, he is being held by—'

'Yes. And this Hedge? You are suggesting that he is in some way connected with Logan?'

'It would appear very possible, Comrade Foreign Minister.'

'Perhaps, yes. What is known of Hedge, Comrade?'

The official opened up a file that he had balanced on his knee. 'Hedge is next in the hierarchy to the Head of Security in the British Foreign Office. He is aged sixty-four and it will be not long before he retires—'

'Expendable?'

'Yes, that is possible. He is known to be anxious for honours from his Queen and that also is perhaps relevant. A last job, with accolades to follow. He is known also to be pompous and conceited. In appearance he is portly and short and dresses conventionally.'

'No cloak, no dagger, no bomb with attached fuse peering from the pocket?' This was a joke; both men laughed. Hedge was not like that, the official said. He referred to the report from the German Democratic Republic. 'He is, he says, a gentleman and that is why he is not a spy.'

The Foreign Minister rose to his feet and went across his large and opulent office to gaze down through a tall window onto the passing Moscow scene, deep beneath hard-packed snow. Men and women stumbled across the icy wastes of the square in the Kremlin's shadow, men and women queued for almost non-existent food and other commodities. There was not a car in sight; this was largely due to the weather but was due also to the terrible shortages that had so sadly continued even after the advent of the good Comrade Gorbachev and new freedoms. Shortages of this, that and the other, shortage of money among the lower echelons of communism. *Glasnost* had not in all truth made a very great deal of difference, at any rate internally—except that it had hastened the aspirations of the people in the various republics towards self-determination. The riots that there had been! It was alarming; and it was also relevant to certain things that had been said to be happening. The perfidious West was, so it was rumoured, thinking of taking advantage of the current discomfiture of Comrade Gorbachev...

The Foreign Minister turned from his contemplation of street misery—it had started to snow again now, and the persons in the square had become invisible beneath the cruel, icy shafts of the blizzard—and went back to his desk. He said, 'You are aware of the rumours, Comrade. That the West is thought to be trying to find an excuse to attack the Soviets while we are subject to the distractions of civil unrest. There may be nothing in this. On the other hand...perhaps this Hedge may be persuaded to enlighten us? What do you think, Comrade?'

'I agree, Comrade Foreign Minister, but would make a suggestion regarding Hedge. Before he is brought to Moscow...suppose he were to be released with apologies for a wrongful apprehension?'

'Ah—lulled, do you suggest?'

'Exactly, Comrade Foreign Minister. And then followed.'

'To lead us to who knows what?'

'Yes. And finally arrested, and brought here to Moscow.'

So it was agreed. An excellent suggestion, the Foreign Minister said. It would be better than leaving the whole thing in the hands of the KGB. The KGB was not what once it had been; the KGB had been castrated by the good Comrade Gorbachev.

Hedge was once more brought from his cell and taken before the uniformed thin man. The atmosphere was very different this time and Hedge was overjoyed to learn the reason why.

'I'm very grateful,' he effused.

'We in the East are not as bad as we are shown in the West, Herr Hedge.'

Herr Hedge. Last time it had been just Hedge, very rude really. This man had no doubt been given his come-uppance by his superiors and a very good thing too. But it still behoved Hedge, he supposed, to show some sort of deference—he was still physically in East Germany and he had to get out in one piece, and quickly too. He was becoming out of touch with events and he still had an urgent need to contact Shard. In reference to the thin man's last utterance about not being all that bad, Hedge said, 'No, no, of course not. Of course not. I've *never* gone along with that, you know.'

'No, I did not know.'

'Oh. Well, anyway, I say again, I'm really immensely grateful. If I may have my belongings returned?'

The thin man opened a drawer in his desk and brought out a sealed packet which he handed to Hedge. Hedge opened it and checked the contents. All correct: wallet, shoe-laces, tie, money and keys—braces. Hedge gave a sigh of relief: life had been extremely uncomfortable, at any rate when on the move to and from the thin man's presence.

'Thank you very much,' Hedge said, 'most kind.'

'It is *glasnost*. We are instructed to be—we are always—kind.'

'Oh yes, indeed.' Hedge hesitated. 'Er...am I to be assisted back to Berlin?'

'No.'

'I see. But really. I do think—in the circumstances—'

'No.'

'—of my wrongful arrest,' Hedge ploughed on, 'that it's only—'

'No. That will not be possible.'

So they were not being that kind. The interview was at an end; the thin man stood up. He held out a bony hand, which Hedge took. 'Good morning, Herr Hedge,' the thin man said. The guards, who were there still by the door, took Hedge to another room where he clipped his braces back onto his trousers. Then with his greatcoat also returned he was shown to the exit and stepped out into freedom.

Snow was falling thickly and it was very cold.

'Logan.'

'Schreuder. I am Schreuder. But of course you knew that. Logan suited my purpose all those years ago.'

'When you were in England,' Shard said. 'Acting for the Germans.'

'Yes. For my own country. For Hitler.'

'Are you still for Hitler?'

'Yes.' The voice was strong now, filled with a kind of passion, a deep loyalty to a dead murderer. 'My loyalties have never changed, neither have my beliefs. I'm not like some others who fear their fate too much.'

Shard said nothing. With Logan/Schreuder he was sheltering in a barn, or not exactly a barn he believed—more like one of the outlying buildings, storehouses for animal feedstuffs, that dotted some of the North Yorkshire dales, a long way from any other buildings. Back behind the house that had caught fire, he'd had some luck. Brosak's mistake in opening fire had rebounded in Shard's favour; the shots had been heard and a posse of armed police had come round from the front, shining large torches. Brosak had turned and run; the police, giving chase, hadn't seen Shard and Logan, still flattened to the ground. Shard hadn't seen what happened subsequently to Brosak and his thugs; but as soon as it was safe to do so he had struck out into the countryside, more or less carrying Logan, and had found their shelter.

Logan, who seemed better, the apparently imminent heart attack not having materialised, spoke again. 'We can't stay here long, you know. They'll—'

'Agreed.' It was a long way yet to the dawn; they would move out soon, taking advantage of the darkness. But where to? Shard asked, 'You want to get back to West Germany, Schreuder?'

'Of course. And you?'

Shard laughed. 'Likewise! Do you know the terrain round here?'

'A little, but many years ago. Before the partition, you see. There will have been many changes, obviously.'

Shard nodded. He said, 'Before we move out, there are some questions.'

'I am sure, there are, my friend. But why ask them now? Wouldn't it be better to concentrate on getting out of this vile country?' Suddenly he gave a quiet laugh. 'Or do you fear that I shall die before you have another opportunity? If so, I shall set your mind at rest. I shall not die. And I shall not answer any questions. For your part, you are depending on me to get you out. So there will be no violence.' Logan laughed again. 'But this much I'll tell you, Mr Shard: matters are moving to a climax now, all is ready. And there are certain people in your country, people in high places, who will ensure that—let us say, certain things will be done when they know that I am still in the land of the living.'

Shard said no more. Logan's voice had been filled with hate; hate for the British, for the East Germans, for all who were opposed to the concept of Adolf Hitler. For the sake of that dead monster Logan was, as Shard knew, prepared to see the world plunged again into war. A moment later Logan confirmed this.

He said, 'If you British don't act while Russia is caught by her own difficulties, then your country will die. That is very certain. And I believe this is known in Whitehall.'

The rabies, of course. Shard asked, 'How do you go about giving the word, Logan—Schreuder? Currently, you're not in any position to communicate?'

Logan was fully confident. He was not

alone, he said; and, always with half an eye on possible abduction or capture, he had left instructions where they would be carried out to the letter.

In the north of England a police mobile, driving down from Middleton-in-Teesdale to Brough along the B6276, observed a helicopter flying low from east to west over the big reservoir at Grassholme. The helicopter carried the markings of the Army Air Corps and the constables in the mobile thought nothing of it. Neither did they remark upon a car stopped on the road that crossed the reservoir, or upon a man who had got out of the car and was standing contemplating the water. It was nothing out of the ordinary; the mobile went on and of course no report was made. Like all police forces nationwide, the constables were well aware of the rabies threat and they were still keeping an eye open for dog compounds and the like, if with somewhat decreasing vigilance. And they knew that to get rabies you needed to be bitten by infected teeth. Rabies had no connection with helicopters or reservoirs or solitary men getting out of cars...

Farther south in Bedfordshire, a man

with a canvas bag slung over his shoulder also got out of a car and walked towards a reservoir. He too was observed by a passing mobile; but he was only a fisherman. What was there to look at twice?

Again—no interest. Which was a pity as things were to turn out.

Hedge trudged through the appalling day, the terrible snow. At times it was like walking on ice. He was trying to find transport; anything would do—the bus, the train, even a taxi if the driver would take him all the way to Berlin. There was not a taxi to be seen, however; and at the bus station, when he found it more or less by accident—having enquired the way but not fully understanding the answer and the stupid German arm-waving—no buses seemed to be running; he didn't know why and there was no-one around to ask. A public holiday, perhaps? But in the East they didn't particularly celebrate Christmas. A strike? They didn't, or they didn't used to, countenance strikes in the Eastern Bloc, which of course was a point in their favour. Or had been.

Behind Hedge, at a safe distance, trudged two plain-clothes policemen. Like

Hedge themselves, they were cold, soon tired, for Hedge's way was long, and bloody-minded as to their current duty. Their quarry was scarcely behaving suspiciously; tiredly only. The Englishman's gait suggested that he suffered badly from corns; or perhaps flat feet only.

They became alert each time Hedge stopped to speak to somebody; but in the end came to the conclusion, the correct one, that he was merely asking the way. To somewhere. They cogitated; a rendezvous, or a way out of Dresden? Time perhaps would tell.

Ahead of the two plain-clothes men, Hedge entered an eating establishment. The followers strolled to the other side of the street and watched, casually, from the pavement—watched by studying the reflection in the window of a shop that sold marital aids. The policemen stared at but did not see—for they were concentrating on the reflections of Hedge—an interesting assortment of gadgets. From inside, the shopkeeper, a stout man with a heavy moustache and liver-yellow eyes, watched the men. They were clearly police. Their eyes appeared to bore through his window display and see other things that it were better they should not see. The shopkeeper went away deeper into his premises and made sure that his pornographic literature was secure where it would not easily be found.

Inside the café Hedge sat in a steamy atmosphere along with two workmen and a sluttish-looking woman in a dirty head-scarf.

He ordered only coffee and a roll; the food in his cell had been atrocious, scarcely eatable in fact, but he was not really hungry: he was too worried, too upset altogether. He was not supposed to be in the field to this extent; he was the co-ordinator supposedly static in the Berlin Consulate-General. That he was here in Dresden was, he admitted to himself, his own fault. To a large extent anyway: that Berlin store and Father Christmas—and that wretched girl and her taxi—must share some of the blame. Also the sugar-beet lorry. But how was he convincingly to explain to the Permanent Under-Secretary that so many things had come together to frustrate him? He still believed that Father Christmas had been Logan. And now Father Christmas would be dispersed for another year, his season being over.

The coffee and roll came: having consumed that he tendered British currency, his West German cash having all been expended on his taxi in Berlin. This the proprietor didn't like. There was an argument; the German grew heated and abusive—he spoke no English, but all his meanings were crystal clear. Hedge said he was very sorry but the sterling currency was all he could manage. The fact of his Englishness was another source of anger to the Democratic German and there was a threat of the police being called. Hedge didn't understand half of all this and got to his feet with dignity, making for the exit. The proprietor followed, shouting, laying hands on Hedge as he emerged into the snow.

Across the street, the two plain-clothes men swung round. They took in the gist of the loudly-conducted dispute; their eyes met. Without money, negotiable money, their quarry would be brought to a dead stop and nothing would be learned about him. They also heard the shouted threat of the police, and there would be little point in allowing the Englishman to be at this stage returned to the custody from whence he had come.

They crossed the street. They spoke in English. 'Your pardon, *mein Herr*. We happened to hear,' one of them said. 'You will permit us to be of assistance, *hein?*'

Hedge was astonished. He stared at some notes in the hand of the plain-clothes man. 'It's awfully decent of you. But why—'

'It is the wish of all Germans to increase and assist the tourism. That is of much importance to our country, the good relationship with all people. Please accept.' The money was thrust into Hedge's not unwilling palm. His fingers closed over it, and he uttered thanks. The British Embassy would repay, he said, and did they want a receipt?

No receipt was required. The café proprietor uttered noises and was paid. Hedge enquired the way to the railway station. He set off and the plain-clothes men walked at a distance behind. Since their personal usefulness was now at an end, the senior of them used a small radio and spoke to headquarters, giving the current known destination of the Englishman. Two fresh plain-clothes men would pick up the suspect at the railway station.

By this time all the police forces of the Western continental nations were on the watch for Logan. Also for Detective Chief Superintendent Shard. In Whitehall there was much concern about what might have happened to Shard, now out of communication for a considerable period. Again a meeting of the Cabinet had been called. The position appeared to be stalemate. No Logan, no implementation of the threat, no sign of rabies either. The Home Secretary referred again to the earlier Cabinet minutes: the whole thing could be a bluff, though he was unable to make any suggestion as to why there should be a bluff. It all seemed totally without point.

This time the Prime Minister disagreed, sensing *ennui* amongst the Cabinet members. There was surely substance; undoubtedly Shard had disappeared, undoubtedly Hedge was in Communist hands. Why—if there was no substance?

'Let us recap, shall we?'

There were nods. 'Yes, Prime Minister.'

'Very well. Logan proposes to *wipe out* us British by the use of this new and very rapid strain of rabies. This he will do unless we, with America, go into immediate action against the USSR. This sounds totally crazy—I think we're all agreed on that, and all agreed that Logan is nothing short of a madman. But I ask you to remember that *many times* throughout history, madmen have succeeded in their enterprises against *all sane likelihood.*' Mrs Heffer thumped the table. 'Although nothing further has been heard from Logan, I believe we must still take this threat seriously, as I've said all along. It is true what Logan has said: the Soviets are in a state of disarray, wide open to a concerted attack. The concept—while unthinkable of course—is not wholly impossible.'

There were nods. The Defence Secretary asked, 'Has there been any shift in the American position, Prime Minister?'

There had not. There had been another transatlantic conversation, Prime Minister to President. The President had been adamant. Also angry and impatient.

'For God's sake! Do you seriously mean to suggest that we're likely to agree to go into a pre-emptive strike on the say-so of a guy who clearly needs his goddamn head read?'

'The rabies, George—'

'Hasn't happened.'

'Yet, George. Yet.'

'And won't! It's a load of baloney. If it did happen...'

'Yes?'

The President had seemed to react. 'No comment. I'm sorry Charlotte, but you British, you're over-reacting. The whole thing's *wacky.*'

'Suppose it was the US?' the Prime Minister said.

'Well, if it was, then I guess we'd deal with it. Find the source, find the goddamn dogs—you know?'

It was useless; Mrs Heffer had cut the call in a huff. When told of the American response, the Cabinet was collectively unsurprised. Nevertheless, the Defence Secretary reported that if lunacy did prevail, then he was as ready as was possible. War, in these times, could in fact be mounted very quickly. There was little need, despite what he had said earlier, to call up reserves or make large-scale troop movements. The RAF was always on an alert, always ready, as were the nuclear submarines on their deep, silent and secret patrols. The missiles could be sent off within seconds of a Prime

Ministerial decision. All armed services were already, just as a normal precaution, on an amber alert.

Mrs Heffer made a classic final comment: 'Of course, it *may never* happen.' But she clearly didn't believe that.

In a state of nerves for one reason and another, the members dispersed back to their ministries. In some of their hearts, Logan was still very much a time-bomb. There had not yet been a full investigation of the suicide of one of their colleagues, but when that did happen some very dirty washing could be revealed. Of course, it was always possible to engineer a cover-up if the matter remained internal, but while Logan lived it would not remain internal. In some of the ministerial breasts there lurked a deep and so-far hidden thought: back in the thirties, Adolf Hitler had been appeased. Perhaps now it would be as well to appease Logan...

Shard was not prepared to move in the full light of day. The East German police would be much too vigilant and the geriatric Logan would stand out a mile. Also, his disappearance would most probably be known to Moscow; and the KGB would be baying however discreetly at the heels of the East German authorities. A failure to find and apprehend Logan would lead to some very harsh recriminations.

The day following the overnight trek eastwards from the barn-like building was endured in a long-abandoned railway siding where there stood a truck that looked as though it hadn't been used for many years. It stood rusted and silent and empty amid the snow. Shard approached it with extreme caution and never mind the fact that the whole surrounding area appeared deserted and abandoned. There were small, mean houses nearby, now with all windows heavily boarded over, once probably the homes of railwaymen. Logan, who was looking unwell again, had wanted to try to enter one of the houses but Shard had refused. Signs of a break-in would attract attention if any police patrols came around. The truck would provide all the shelter they could afford currently. They clambered aboard, entering through a sliding door that stood half open. Shard assisted Logan through, and the old man, breathing heavily, sank to the filthy, rotted floorboards, moaning to himself now. For most of the journey towards the Western sector he had talked, a continuous outpouring of hatred for what had been the Allied Powers in the war, castigating the leaders of old, Churchill and Roosevelt and de Gaulle, for not having done the sensible thing, which would have been to throw in their lot with the Führer and the Third Reich, a combination of enormous strength that would have ruled the world. There would have been eternal peace world-wide; over-ridingly, the Soviets would have been forever impotent, the great land mass ruled from Berlin, London and Washington. The West, Logan kept on saying, had missed its great opportunity and now he was handing it back to them.

'By way of threat,' Shard said harshly. Logan was, he'd found, a loathsome man, acid, sadistic in his outlook—the man had gloried in what Hitler had done to the Jews—swayed by his Nazi past to a point of irretrievable insanity. If it hadn't been for Hedge, Shard would have considered handing Logan over to the East Germans, who would quickly have dealt with any threat. But Hedge was under threat from his London kidnappers...and whatever Hedge had done in the past,

Shard's loyalty would not allow him to go back on his word, to say nothing of his duty as instructed, to bring Logan back to the West.

Logan began coughing again, as he had back in the burning house. It was a racking sound; the journey through the snow had been bad. Logan's face had a nasty flush, but as Shard watched, the flush faded and was replaced by a grey pallor. Shard did what he could; it wasn't much. He removed his own jacket and rolled it up, placing it beneath the old man's head. That head was square, Prussian. A bitter wind swept in through the door. The door was heavily rusted and Shard had been unable to close it further and it remained half open. Snow came in on the wind. Shard had dragged Logan to one end of the truck, in the lee of the sides, but if the snow and the wind direction continued there was going to be drifting inside the truck.

He would not move out until nightfall. It was going to be a long day. Logan fell into a kind of sleep, a very disturbed one. His limbs moved restlessly and he jabbered away to himself, something rooted in the great days of the 'thirties when Adolf

Hitler's star had been in the ascendant. When at last the rambling stopped, Logan lifted his head and focused on Shard. 'What day is it?' he asked.

Shard told him.

'And the time?'

'1030 hours,' Shard said. 'Why do you ask, Logan?'

Logan laughed; the sound was more like a cackle. 'I wanted to know how much longer was left.'

Shard said nothing, waiting for Logan. Logan went on, 'I am going to die, do you know that?'

'I thought you said—'

'I know what I said. But I feel it now. I begin to see my Führer...more clearly. And I have to tell you now...when I die, my life's work will not die with me. There are those who are pledged to carry it on.'

'Brosak?'

'Yes. Brosak will...' The voice faded, once again Logan closed his eyes. Shard reminded him that he had wanted to know the time and date so that he would know how much time was left.

'Yes,' Logan said.

'And that—'

'There is a little over three days left, my

215

friend. Three days for the West to agree to what I have demanded, and if they do not, then...' The voice faded away again.

Shard prompted. 'The rabies, Logan?'

Logan laughed again. 'Not the rabies. There was no rabies. There is no new strain, no speeded-up proliferation of the disease.'

'It was all bluff, Logan?'

'Oh, no, no! Not bluff. Merely a ploy to distract your security people in the wrong direction. I tell you this now, because shortly your government will also be told...when it is too late. It's all ready now.' Logan paused; his eyes were very bright as he stared at Shard through the blinding snow, and there was hate and triumph mixed in his voice as he went on. 'Not rabies. Botulin. Botulin, in all the reservoirs throughout Britain.'

11

At the railway station Hedge had made an important discovery: there was no train for Berlin until very late that evening; this was due to an unprecedentedly heavy fall of snow along the track. This would take time to clear; and this was not all. Trees had been brought down across the railway line owing to the weight of the snow, a great many of them. The booking clerk spoke a little English, and had been able to convey this information. Hedge thanked him, and moved disconsolately about the windswept tracks, in and out of an empty waiting room—there were no other intending passengers—that he found bleak and bare. There was another problem: money. The notes given him by the kind men outside the café were not sufficient for the fare, so he had bought no ticket. As a result he was in a dilemma as to how he was to board the train, because the booking clerk would know he was without a ticket. But he believed he could overcome that, with luck. He had been told the train was likely to be a long one and the end coaches might not come right into the station proper. He should be able to move right to the end, get down by the track, and climb aboard, heaving himself up onto the running-board and opening a door. He was unworried as to what would happen on arrival ticketless; he was also unworried about security checks as the train entered Berlin. There were two reasons for this lack of worry: one, he would be close to the safety of the Consulate-General whose officials would not only vouch for him but would also send money for the ticket and provide a car to bring him to the safety he found, now, that he couldn't wait for. And two, there was absolutely nothing else he could do in any case, no alternative that he would need to ponder. Walking the station in misery, Hedge sent a prayer upwards through the falling snow and then once again retreated to the horrible bareness of the waiting room.

The booking clerk had imparted train information not only to the Englishman but also to two men who produced their police identity cards. Yes, the Englishman had enquired about the trains to Berlin. No, he had not bought a ticket.

'Yet he is still here.'

'He is still here, yes. He intends, I think, to wait for the train's arrival.'

'To wait all day?'

'If he wishes to reach Berlin, he will have to wait all day,' the booking clerk said with a touch of malice. He didn't like the English, he had read much about lager louts and abominable behaviour at international football matches and although the Englishman had not looked like a lager lout you couldn't always go by appearances. The booking clerk had read in his newspapers that English stockbrokers and city businessmen and lawyers and accountants were accustomed to getting drunk on leaving their offices and laid about themselves when boarding the suburban trains and molested the undrunk female passengers.

The plain-clothes men thanked him. 'Say nothing, do you understand, to the Englishman?'

They then retreated out of the railway station, conferring together, huddling against the snow in a doorway down the road from the station buildings. One of them used his radio; orders came back that they were to remain in the vicinity and watch the Englishman as before, a cold and unwelcome vigil but necessary for the security of the state.

While the men watched, communication was made with the Russian sector of Berlin; East Berlin in turn communicated with Moscow. In Moscow it was considered that Hedge had no present intention of contacting suspicious persons but if he was allowed to reach Berlin then very likely he would be forever lost to the East—there would be jiggery-pokery from the British Consul-General, obviously.

That evening, the train from Dresden to Berlin left without Hedge aboard.

Logan had been right: while Hedge shivered in the Dresden railway station, and while Shard waited for night-time in the derelict truck, word reached Whitehall by a telephone call from an unknown source. The caller, a man, spoke good English but there was an obvious German accent. The message was brief and was conveyed at once to the Prime Minister.

'Botulin!'

'Yes, Prime Minister.' The Home Secretary was making the report by the security line from the Home Office. 'In every one of our reservoirs and their ancillary...er...pumping stations and so on. I—'

'They'll never get away with it, they can't *possibly!* Not now we've been warned.'

'Prime Minister...they wouldn't have sent the warning unless they felt certain we couldn't circumvent their plans—'

'Well, I don't know about that, Walter. They'd surely need to give us time—time to consider their demands—time to *concede,* if that was what we decided upon. Not that we *would,* of course. What was that?' The Home Secretary had muttered something indistinct.

'I said this is a very different threat from rabies, Prime Minister. I don't think any of us really believed in the rabies. Too cumbersome, too slow in spite of what Logan seemed to be claiming. And none of those compounds existed, and only the one case—that Scottish policeman, and quite unconnected. But botulin! In all the reservoirs! Our whole population at immediate risk the moment they drank a glass of water—'

'Water can be boiled, surely?'

'Certainly, Prime Minister. But I already have a summary before me of the effects of botulism.' The Home Secretary paused and read some of it out. ' "The spores are very highly resistant to heat. They can withstand a hundred degrees centigrade for some three to four hours." There would be bound to be a spread, it would be absolutely inevitable. I do think this alters the situation, Prime Minister.'

'H'm. To the point of war with the Soviet Union, Walter?'

'A very difficult thing to suggest to the nation, of course.'

'There would be no question of suggesting it, Walter,' Mrs Heffer said with asperity. '*I* would decide and the *general public* would find out later. One does not govern by asking the people first. However, I take your point. And I do *not* propose to concede *anything*, Walter. Now, tell me more about botulin.'

There were few toxins more virulent, more lethal than botulin. Found chiefly in soil and animal faeces, material which was naturally very widespread, it was not welcome in water supplies. Something like an egg-cupful of the spores could contaminate an entire reservoir of great size. There were seven distinct antigenic varieties, categorised A-G. A, B, and E were associated chiefly with human illness; inter alia, C produced limberneck in fowl, D produced botulism in cattle.

'Do come to the *point*, Walter,' Mrs Heffer said impatiently.

'Yes, Prime Minister.'

The Home Secretary proceeded with his painstaking exposition. The category to be used by Logan could be presumed to be either A or B or E. The lethal human dose was about one to two ugs.

'Ugs?'

'Micrograms, Prime Minister.'

'I see. Go on.'

The toxin, the Home Secretary said, acted by blocking the release of acetyl-choline at synapses and neuromuscular junctions. The result to the human body was flaccid paralysis. The symptoms would commence from eighteen to ninety-six hours after ingestion. 'Drinking the water,' the Home Secretary put in helpfully and there was an exclamation of annoyance down the line. Visual disturbances would be noticed—incoordination of the eye muscles, and double vision—and there would come an inability to swallow, plus speech difficulty. Signs of bulbar paralysis would come and these would be progressive to the point of death, which would occur from respiratory paralysis or cardiac arrest. There would be no fever; and the patient would remain fully conscious until on the point of death.

'And the fatality rate, Walter?'

'Extremely high, Prime Minister—'

'Yes. Now then: what about the *cure?*'

There was a pause. 'Guanidine hydrochloride should be given, Prime Minister, and respiration should be artificially maintained—'

'The kiss of life?'

'I expect so, Prime Minister, but since a whole household and even a whole community would be affected together—'

'Yes, all right, Walter.'

'I suggest we contact the Communicable Diseases Control Centre in Colindale, Prime Minister, for further advice.'

'Yes, good thinking, Walter, do that immediately. Get the Department of Health onto them. Is there anything else, anything we can do to *lessen the effects* if not provide a *cure?*'

'Well...there is salt, Prime Minister.'

'*Salt?* Ordinary salt?'

'Yes. A high concentration of salt does in fact diminish the spores' resistance to heat.'

The Prime Minister pounced on that. 'So boiling the water would become a possibility, an *effective* possibility, Walter?'

'As I understand it, yes, Prime Minister.'

'Good.' The wretched Nazi, Logan, was not going to get his way. Salt would be the salvation. The British public would put up with salty water and a lot of boiling rather than die or be plunged into war. (Like it or not, they were going to *have* to put up with it.) Mrs Heffer, the call finished, got up and went into her bedroom. She surveyed herself in a long wall mirror, head to foot. She tilted her head and looked quizzically at her hair. Something wrong there, not sufficiently *bouffant.* She fluffed at it, and went back to the telephone to call an urgent meeting of the Cabinet. After that, Buckingham Palace would have to be warned, something Mrs Heffer, considering the seriousness of the situation, would do by personal call, an urgent request for an audience.

In the meantime—salt. Mrs Heffer

clicked her tongue in self-annoyance: she should have been explicit with Walter. She called him back and the salt operation was put into immediate effect. Orders went out from the appropriate ministries for all possible salt supplies to be collected and distributed to all reservoirs throughout the country. This order included all the dumps of salt deposited along the road network for use in freezing conditions. As a first result, by that evening, there had been a series of nasty accidents in Cumbria and Northumberland and other places and the A66 from Scotch Corner to Penrith and the M6 were closed to traffic as was the road over Shap Fell and a number of lesser roads chiefly in the north.

Orders had also gone out that the reservoirs were to be closely watched by ground patrols and by helicopters, and any lurkers arrested immediately and questioned. But in Mrs Heffer's mind something else, something very sinister and worrying, lurked: another telephone call, one that had come in urgently from the Commissioner of Metropolitan Police subsequent to that from the Home Secretary and Mrs Heffer's summoning of the Cabinet. That call had gone to Scotland Yard from Brosak.

Brosak was out of East Germany now.

He had written Logan off. Logan had vanished along with Shard. Logan wouldn't talk, of course, but it was unlikely he would take any further part in the action. That didn't matter now; he, Brosak, was fully briefed and could carry the thing through on his own. It had just been a question of some telephone calls, already made. For a start he had made one to a woman, a German woman married to an Englishman living in Carlisle in Cumbria. The call was brief.

'Stand by, Lotte,' was all Brosak said. The woman understood and within half an hour had made three telephone calls of her own. To the West Country, to the Peak District, and to mid-Wales. From various houses other men and women set out in their cars.

Some hours later, after taking a call in West Berlin, a call from Carlisle, Brosak was back again on the telephone. This was his call to Scotland Yard, urgent and personal to the Commissioner. He was asked who he was. 'I speak for Logan,' he said. *'Heil, Hitler!'* That was when the Commissioner reported to the

Prime Minister direct.

'He says it's all ready, Prime Minister. His agents had no difficulty in getting past the foot patrols. Considering the sheer size of the operation, the sheer extent of the reservoirs, that's scarcely surprising. The lads can't be everywhere at once.'

'So the supplies are already contaminated?' Mrs Heffer asked.

'Not contaminated yet, no. Plastic bags...not quite plastic, some sort of material that will melt in forty-eight hours and release the spores. Just one small bag in each reservoir.'

'So we have just forty-eight hours?'

'Rather less, Prime Minister. It'll take Brosak's people two or three hours, he says, to fish the bags out again.'

'I see. Once we've conceded?'

'Yes, that's it in a nutshell,' the Commissioner said.

'Thank you *very* much,' Mrs Heffer snapped, and banged the receiver down hard. 'Roly?'

'Yes, Prime Minister?'

'Contact Defence Ministry. They're to be ready instantly.'

The Foreign Secretary looked perturbed.

'Does this mean you're conceding, Prime Minister?'

Mrs Heffer's eyes flashed. 'I *never* concede *anything*, Foreign Secretary, but it might be as well to let this man Brosak *think* I'm conceding. If you follow.'

'Ah. But is there not an element of danger in doing that, Prime Minister.'

'There is *always* danger,' Mrs Heffer said, 'whenever anyone tries to do *anything positive*. Apart from that—'

'I'm thinking of Hedge, you see, Prime Minister.'

'As I—Hedge?' Mrs Heffer looked baffled.

'Yes, my man Hedge. In—'

'Ah—yes, I'm with you, Roly.' Mrs Heffer caught a glimpse of her hair, reflected from the glass of a large picture opposite where she sat. Still not quite right... 'Hedge, such a gallant man. In Germany. What about him?'

'He's in East German hands still, Prime Minister.'

'Yes. That's most unfortunate, of course.'

'If there's any strike, then I would much fear for Hedge's safety—'

'I *never* suggested a strike. Don't put words into my mouth, Roly. I said merely that I shall allow this man Brosak to *think* I may concede. That's all.'

'So that he retrieves those bags, Prime Minister?'

Mrs Heffer gave a snort of derision. 'Really, Roly, do you suppose *for one moment* that anyone, any vile person such as this—this *Brosak* seems to be, would remove this threat until he was certain he'd got what he wanted?'

Rowland Mayes took the point. 'Yes, well, quite, Prime Minister, I do see...yes.' He paused. 'But in that case why—'

'Leave the details to me, Roly, me and the police. And the armed services. We shall cope, you may be quite certain of that.'

'Yes, Prime Minister. But I believe the effect on my man Hedge will be much the same as if you really did intend to mount a strike against the Eastern—'

'Possibly, though I don't see why. But Hedge must simply do his duty, that's all. I'm sorry, of course...*genuinely* sorry, to put any man, any *patriot,* in such danger, but it simply can't be helped. I feel *quite certain* your Mr Hedge will understand.' Mrs Heffer looked at her watch and clicked her tongue. 'Roly, you'll have to excuse me now. I'm due at the Palace. To give reassurance, you know—the poor Queen's distracted by all this, naturally enough, I suppose. I shall do my best to set her mind at rest without playing down the terrible *seriousness* of the situation.'

'Yes, Prime Minister.' The Foreign Secretary gathered up his papers and stuffed them back into his briefcase, the look of dog-like devotion on his face slipping just a little. No doubt it was perfectly right and proper that Her Majesty should receive preference from her Prime Minister, but Mrs Heffer had seemed to cut him off somewhat abruptly and he had intended making a reference to Detective Chief Superintendent Shard, also still missing and presumed to be in East Germany, and also at much risk if Great Britain should be thought—even just thought—to be marching as to war.

The helicopters, Royal Navy, Army Air Corps, RAF and police, flew on their anti-botulin sweeps over the reservoirs. The police mobiles kept their watch closely—or as closely as possible.

A few fishermen were seen and apprehended. They were all in the clear. There was the odd tramp, also innocent so far as the police could tell. There were no lurkers as such, no persons of apparent evil intent. Piles of salt, brought by fleets of lorries that clogged the roads, were dumped beside the reservoirs and cast into the water by men with spades and in some cases by machines that spewed the salt out from metal mouths at the ends of big long necks, like horses being sick. These had been commandeered from the farming community. The farmers, the sheep and cattle and pig men, were much concerned about water for their livestock. The poultry farmers and those with hens in batteries would be on the watch for limberneck.

Hedge had been picked up during a very long afternoon. While he had been cogitating about how best to conceal himself when the train should eventually come along—conceal his intention to board, or perhaps it would be better to ride the buffers or something, which he understood was a ploy much used in the Eastern Bloc—he was approached by two men, plain-clothes men. Not the ones of the morning.

One spoke to him, using laboured English. 'You are Hedge?'

'Yes—yes I am.' Despite the cold, Hedge broke out into a sweat of sheer relief. Help at last—money, perhaps, for his ticket to Berlin and civilisation, the police having perhaps been instructed. 'Are you from police HQ?'

'Yes. We—'

'You've come to my assistance?'

'Yes, we—'

'I call that very decent of you. You simply don't know how very relieved and grateful I am.'

'Yes. You will come with us, please.'

'Yes, of course. Thank you. Somewhere more comfortable until the train comes in.'

There was no response to that; but the men smiled and one of them took his arm. The grip was not entirely friendly, Hedge felt. Alarm stirred; outside the railway station a police car waited. Hedge was steered towards this and thrust into the back. The two men got in, one on either side of him. The car was driven away fast. It entered the courtyard of the police HQ from which he had been so thankfully discharged that morning. He had asked en route, fearful of the answer, if he was going to be taken to Berlin by road.

'*Nein,*' the plain-clothes spokesman had said.

Now there was alarm throughout the country. The Prime Minister, knowing very well that the threat could not remain hidden, had spoken once again on TV to the people, giving them the facts of the botulin. (Straight from the shoulder and in personal appearance, she had said in Cabinet, not trusting the press to get it right. However, she intended saying nothing about the alternative, which was Logan's ridiculous wish for a strike against the Soviet Union.)

In Cabinet everyone had had his or her say. There were those who believed that Logan would win, that war would become inevitable, however horrendous a prospect that might be.

'Not if we catch Logan,' Mrs Heffer said firmly. 'Logan's the key figure. And we have men in the field who may well be on his track even now. Roly?'

Rowland Mayes, Foreign Secretary, looked up, sleeked his hair down with one hand. 'Yes, Prime Minister?'

'Is there any word of progress, Roly?'

'I'm afraid not, Prime Minister. Nothing's been heard from our men in Germany. Except, as you know, that Hedge is in East German hands.'

'Not very propitious, Roly.'

'No, Prime Minister.' The Foreign Secretary furrowed his brow in a nervous frown. 'Prime Minister...this botulin. I was wondering what's come through from the Communicable Diseases people in—'

'Nothing that's of much help.' Mrs Heffer looked annoyed. 'Have you a suggestion, Roly?'

'Well, I thought—the Guy's Hospital Poison Unit may have some ideas.'

Mrs Heffer sighed. 'Botulism isn't a poison, Roly. It's a disease. The two things are *quite* different.'

'Yes, but—'

'It's not your department, Roly. Foreign Affairs *are*. So is finding Logan. Finding him *in time.*'

'Yes, Prime Minister.' Rowland Mayes subsided, looking hurt. Mrs Heffer had had a decided edge to her voice in that last exchange and he was only doing his best to help in a terrible situation. And Mrs Heffer seemed to be putting all her faith—if the worst came to the worst and Logan went into action—in the distribution of salt and the boiling of water. Which, he had to admit, was possibly all she *could* do.

'Boiling water, I ask you!' Mrs Micklem spoke disparagingly. 'How do you boil a bath, for heaven's sake?'

'By turning up the heat control, mother.'

'I doubt if that would be enough. I've read about botulin. In some magazine or other, an article by a doctor. And you can get water in your mouth when bathing, you know that.' She added, 'What about Stevie?'

Beth let out a long breath. 'I don't know, mother. I really don't. Let's just be content that the government's doing all it can. There's nothing we can do about it anyway. Except perhaps don't bath until it's all over. Not even wash.'

Mrs Micklem made a face. But she said, 'Well, Mrs Heffer's a wonderful lady. If anyone can get us through this, she will, I don't deny.' She paused. 'But I'm ever so worried about little Stevie. You know, Beth, his father ought to be here now, it's his duty.'

'Simon has other duties, mother.'

236

'Yes, well, all right, he has. But nothing's been heard of him since he left, has it?'

Beth stared. 'What's that supposed to mean, mother?'

'Oh, nothing.' Mrs Micklem shrugged. 'Read into it what you like, dear. I never said a thing—'

'Perhaps not, but you were making some kind of suggestion and I wish you wouldn't because I don't damn well like it, mother, when Simon's away—'

'Hoity-toity! We do get upset over nothing, don't we? You're much too quick to react, my girl; anything I say gets taken down in evidence and will be used against me when Simon gets back. Too much of the policeman is rubbing off on you, if you ask me!'

Beth gave it up; there was nothing to be gained from arguing with her mother. She turned away, tears pricking at her eyes, and went up to Stephen's room. The little boy was asleep, clutching a teddy that Simon had bought for him soon after he was born. She looked down at him: so like Simon...if anything should ever happen to Simon...but she knew she mustn't think along those lines, she must be ever optimistic and hopeful or, as a policeman's wife, she would go mad with worry. She was very worried now: it was easy enough to put two and two together. Simon's sudden departure just before Christmas, the total silence from him—the total silence from his immediate boss, Hedge—and now the Prime Ministerial broadcast after all the rumours and the press speculation about a threat to do with rabies. Now it wasn't rabies, it was botulin. And absolutely official too.

Beth saw a clear link between all of that and Simon. The Christmas decorations in Stephen's room, the holly, the ivy, the paper chains and the coloured glass baubles and so on, looked pathetic.

12

It was a long day in the truck. The snow continued to fall. There was plenty of time for thought after Logan had spoken of botulin. There would be no point in Shard abandoning his orders to bring Logan out to the West, no point in going against Hedge in the greater interest of preventing the lethal contamination of Britain's water supplies—it would be easy enough to leave the truck and hand Logan over to the East Germans, but that would not help Britain. The East German government would naturally react against Logan's threat of war, but that would not stop the botulin. Logan would certainly not assist in that.

In the meantime Logan was saying nothing further. He didn't seem in a fit state to. He had already said he was going to die; Shard believed him. And just as dusk was coming down over the thickly lying snow and distantly lights were coming on, Shard realised that Logan was dead.

There were no tears to be shed over that.

But the quarry now was Brosak. And God alone could say where Brosak might be.

At full dark Shard left the comparative shelter of the railway truck and headed towards the lights, not knowing precisely where he was but knowing that it was vital he should reach West Germany and alert security that Brosak had to be located before any distribution of botulin could begin.

After a terrible journey in a very uncomfortable, clapped-out aeroplane, Hedge reached Moscow.

A long black car, very sinister-looking, met him and his East German escort at the airport and he was driven very fast through the appalling snow to the Kremlin. At least the Kremlin was not the Lubyanka prison and this gave Hedge some hope. After all, he was a highly-placed civil servant, a pillar of the Foreign Office if you cared to put it that way, and no doubt he was being taken to meet someone of level importance on the other side.

He was.

240

He was taken along what seemed miles of corridors, even outdoing the British Foreign Office, and deposited in a big chamber with an immensely high ceiling, gilded and painted in the most beautiful colours which he was much too terrified to appreciate. There were big windows, currently with heavy velvet curtains drawn across; the chamber was lit by a number of crystal chandeliers fitted with electric light bulbs in the shape of candles. There was a long, highly-polished mahogany table and at this table sat six men, two of them in plain clothes, four of them in uniform, the uniform of the Soviet Army. Far to one side, in deep shadow, lurked a seventh man, another wearer of plain clothes. Hedge recognised one of the plain-clothes wearers seated at the table—the Russian Foreign Minister, T M Voss, himself. And one of the generals in uniform was the Russian Commander-in-Chief, General Shcherbitsky. Hedge licked nervously at his lips. No-one spoke, but they all looked at him intently, which he didn't like. He knew what they were going to say when they did speak; and he was right.

'You are Hedge.'

'Yes.'

'Of the British Foreign Office.'

'Yes. And I really—'

'Who illegally entered East Germany.'

'Yes. No. Not illegally. By mis—'

'We know all about the sugar-beet lorry.' The speaker was T M Voss; and suddenly, like a switching on of a light, he smiled. 'An unpleasant experience for you,' he said.

'Yes, it was, very. I was quite shaken to find myself—where I did.'

'Which was where you wished to go.'

'No, no,' Hedge corrected with truth. 'I had no intention of entering East Germany, it was a case of *force majeure*, the sugar-beet lorry, you know—'

'Yes. I think we have finished with the sugar-beet lorry, Hedge. There are other and more important things we wished to know from you.'

'I see. Er...what things?'

'Matters of which we know you will be aware—I stress, *know you will be aware.*' T M Voss leaned forward across the polished table; it was so highly polished that it showed T M Voss twice, once in the flesh and again in reflection, which seemed to increase the tension that his office engendered in Hedge, even though the Foreign Minister was smiling still and appeared quite friendly.

T M Voss said, 'I shall not beat about the bush. The matter is most urgent. There is talk of war. Of this, you must of course be aware.'

'Really? I had no idea.'

'Come now, Hedge. You are not a fool. Our intelligence agencies, the men and women who run them, they are not fools either. I say again, we have positive information that your country is contemplating a pre-emptive strike, without warning, against the Soviets. I can tell you that we are quite, quite ready...your country cannot hope to achieve anything—and certainly cannot hope for the element of surprise.' T M Voss turned to the Commander-in-Chief. 'Is this not so, General?'

'It is so,' General Shcherbitsky confirmed. 'The infantry divisions, the artillery, the Air Force, the big missiles. They await the word only.'

'And all this is because of a Nazi, a West German named Logan. And it is because of this that you, Hedge, entered East Germany. We ask you now to tell us the truth, Hedge, so that war may be averted.' T M Voss added after a pause, 'There is not left much time. Tell us, please. We are all friends now. You will be acting for your own country of Great Britain as much as for us. You will be acting for all humanity. If the missiles fly...' T M Voss lifted his shoulders. 'I do not need to tell you how terrible it will be if that happens.'

'No, no. Very terrible—tragic. But really, I don't know anything about all this.'

T M Voss' smile became broader. 'Come now, Hedge, there is no time for verbal play, for stupid denials that will not be believed. You will talk. If you do not...well, I would not advise silence.' He glanced sideways. So did Hedge, following the glance. He saw the man in the shadows, thin, a gaunt face, a rat-trap mouth turning down at the corners, hard eyes, a man who seemed to have the very stench of the Lubyanka about his person, a man who did not have in any way the aura of *glasnost* or *perestroika* about him.

Hedge opened his mouth but no words came. He really didn't know anything that would be of help to the Russians.

Expectantly, they all waited. T M Voss and General Shcherbitsky began to show impatience. The face of the man in the shadows grew gaunter.

Shard had taken a big risk: from outside a sleazy block of flats he had removed a car, a two-stroke Skoda, very anonymous. It was old and clapped-out, not of any value; but it started confidently and he made his getaway. With luck, not too much police time if any would be spared in searching for a banger, but he could still be stopped and questioned. His heart in his mouth whenever he saw a policeman, he drove north-east towards Berlin. Brosak he believed would have got out of East Germany as fast as possible; and without any leads to go on Shard saw Berlin as the best bet, the most likely place for Brosak to make for. Not Rinteln: Brosak wouldn't be taking the risk of going back on his tracks at this stage.

Finding him was Number One priority. But Shard knew the odds were stacked against him. All he could do, he believed, was to do what had often been successful in the past, the ploy of the dick who had no other way to go: make himself into the magnet that would attract the man he wanted. Spread it around...Brosak wouldn't want him on the loose. And if he, Brosak, believed Logan/Schreuder was still alive and with him, that would be an extra magnet.

Driving as fast as the Skoda would make it, which was little enough, watching out for any trouble, Shard hoped the police wouldn't get around to checking that railway wagon too soon. He hadn't been able to dispose of Logan's body, not without risking attracting attention. But it really would be just as well if Brosak didn't know Logan was dead. Not yet.

Having, really, nothing to say, Hedge kept quiet. He could, he supposed, have told the men about the rabies, but they appeared to know that already. They also knew about the Nazi, Logan. Hedge had nothing to add. He could, if they turned really unpleasant, tell them about his own kidnap in London; that would at least show willing and it might distract their attention. Or they might not be in the least interested. Anyway, he would keep that in reserve, some sort of card up his sleeve, a turner away of wrath.

Meanwhile, silence.

The silence lasted quite a long time.

Six pairs of eyes from the front, another pair from the side, bored into Hedge. He became more and more uneasy. They were all like lie-detectors. His mind flitted over many things, once having thought of lie-detectors that mirrored all that went through the victim's mind. Mrs Millington and Mrs Reilly-Jacobs whose name had been mendaciously used by those evil kidnappers; Father Christmas in the West Berlin store; the girl and the taxi and the sugar-beet lorry. He thought of Shard (where, oh where was Shard, who was supposed to be his right-hand man, his saviour in moments of difficulty?) He thought of the Head of Security and the assistant under-secretary.

They would be relying upon him, of course. He was facing his ultimate test for Britain. It was time for stiff upper lips. He tried to steel himself, making a big effort.

He maintained his silence. If he came out of this, that would be sure to stand in his favour, the stout heart that had not given way in the face of threat.

The threat came soon after Hedge had had that thought. Patience was wearing thin, but the threat was politely put, the velvet glove still on the iron fist, part of *perestroika*. It was the gaunt man on Hedge's left who spoke, after a meaningful sideways glance from the Foreign Minister.

'Hedge.'

Hedge started, then turned. 'Yes?'

'Until you speak, Hedge, you will be held in custody. There are two custodies.'

'Really? I see. Two custodies.'

'Two custodies. One, so very nice. Good food and wine, Vodka and Scotch also. A comfortable room with chair, desk and bed. Also a fire—the weather is cold.'

'Yes. Yes, it is, very. Seasonal, of course.'

'Seasonal?'

'Christmas time.'

'Yes. There will also be a woman if you wish.'

'Ah.'

'Or a young man if that is what you prefer.'

'Good heavens, no!' Hedge was suddenly much more alarmed. Was that what they intended—compromising photographs, and a threat that prints would be sent to Whitehall, to Mrs Heffer who would be absolutely scandalised? Once again he said, 'No. Most certainly not!'

The gaunt man shrugged. 'In that case a woman. Also books to read. You understand, Hedge?'

'Yes, I understand. I—I'm grateful.'

'Then there is the other custody.'

'I see.'

'Unless you speak of the things we wish to know. The other custody is unpleasant and there will be no contact with the world outside.' Outside the Lubyanka, Hedge was aware the gaunt man meant. It was Dresden all over again, but worse.

Hedge said what he should have said at the beginning the moment he had arrived inside the Kremlin's terrible walls, made no less terrible by *perestroika*. 'I wish to see the British Ambassador,' he said. 'I must regularise my position, you see.' He had no wish to annoy the faces set before him by being arrogant and demanding at this stage.

'Not possible.' This was the Foreign Minister, T M Voss. 'I am sorry.'

'But it's my right as a British citizen!'

'All rights abrogated,' the Foreign Minister said with finality, 'until questions have been answered.'

'You mean I'm being held prisoner against my will? That's—'

'No, no,' the Foreign Minister said almost amiably. 'You are complying with our requests, that is all. Now, Hedge.' He sat forward, leaning his elbows on the long table and staring hard at Hedge. 'Which of the two custodies is it to be? You will speak in the end, come what may. Why not speak now, and speak in comfort, and remain in comfort until we in the Soviet Union know for certain which way the Western cat will jump?'

It had been a most terrible dilemma. Hedge had brought out his handkerchief, which was a dirty one since he had been accorded no laundry facilities once he had inadvertently left the security of West Berlin, a long time ago now. With the dirty handkerchief he had mopped at his face which had broken out into globules of sweat that ran stickily down into his collar, dirty like the handkerchief. It was, the Foreign Minister said, his simple duty to speak. No-one wished for war; he, Hedge, might be able to prevent it.

'How?' Hedge asked helplessly, his mouth sagging open.

The Foreign Minister shrugged. 'By telling us of the British plans, the Western

250

Alliance plans, if Logan's scheme is not circumvented. You must see that your British interests are the same in basis as our Russian interest. Does this not make sense?'

'Well—yes. Yes, it does, I suppose.' There might well be truth in that. If he, Hedge, could actually prevent a war then he would be honoured on his return to Whitehall. He might perhaps prevent a war by in effect spiking the West's guns—if the Soviet was ready for war, then presumably Mrs Heffer would see that she had lost the element of surprise and that war would be suicidal as well as electorally unsound; she would certainly be very much aware of the election soon to come. Hedge began to see salvation: if he had known Mrs Heffer's plans in detail he really believed he would have blurted them all out. Elation vanished: the fact remained that he didn't know them.

However, he might be able to bluff things out. For a while at least. Until the wretched Logan was caught, anyway, which should be for long enough. After that, he was sure to be released. The Russians had changed a great deal recently.

'Well, Hedge?'

Hedge mopped at his face again. 'If I may have a little time...to co-ordinate my thoughts, you know. This is no light matter for me, you must surely understand that.'

The Foreign Minister nodded. 'Yes. We are an understanding people. Since I believe now that you will co-operate when you have thought, you will be permitted to leave us. For thought.'

'In custody?'

'In custody, of course.'

Hedge scarcely dared ask the question, so fearful was he of the wrong answer. 'The comfortable custody?'

'Yes, the comfortable custody. For the time being. I think you will understand.' The Foreign Minister got to his feet. The others rose as well and all filed out of the chamber behind their leader. The gaunt man, emerging now from his shadows, remained behind. So did the armed guards who had escorted Hedge into the room earlier and who had remained behind his chair throughout the interview. The gaunt man made a signal and the men fell in, one at each side of Hedge. The gaunt man gave him a prod in the back and he got on the move between his escort. He was led along a number of corridors and up two flights of stairs. The building was a very splendid one, still redolent of the days of the czars. Hedge found something reassuring in that, even though those old days were long gone. It was all so very civilised; nothing barbaric at all. He would probably make out all right.

But what was he going to tell the Foreign Minister?

He would need to think very quickly indeed. The point had been made that time was running out fast.

13

Shard ditched the car on the outskirts of East Berlin. He'd been lucky; no police checks. But he wasn't going to push his luck too far, certainly not to the extent of making any attempt to drive through into the Western sector of the city.

How, then, to get in?

He mingled with the crowds, trudging through the snow that fell still and added to the gloom. By this time he was desperately hungry; he had kept thirst more or less at bay by filling his mouth with snow; but he dared not risk going into a café for a meal.

He trudged on towards the crossing into West Berlin, shouldering through the crowds. After a long walk he found himself coming up to Unter den Linden. Passing by a shop, Shard caught sight of his own reflection in the plate glass. Scruffy from his journeyings and from the dirt of the railway track, unshaven, haggard from lack of food, he looked like anyone else in the eastern zone. Nothing about him to stand out, nothing to attract any special attention. Just one of many that morning, walking in Unter den Linden. One of the depressed army of the poor, of which there were still many.

He moved away from the main thorough-fare, making for the meaner streets that lay behind the facade. Into the working areas, where in the courtyards at the back lorries were delivering such merchandise as was available.

There was more than the one way for a person without papers to get through the emasculated entries into West Berlin.

Throughout Britain the reservoirs were being dragged in a desperate attempt to locate and remove Logan's lethal bags. Men also searched and probed with poles and nets from power boats. It was mainly a police operation with the advice and assistance of the various water authorities; but the army and navy were there too. Divers from Fort Blockhouse, the diving school and submarine depot at Gosport in Hampshire. Royal Marines from Eastney and Devonport, wearing commando gear and looking ready for anything. Infantry units turned into probers for plastic bags.

Nothing was found.

This was reported at intervals to the various area control headquarters that had been set up around the country under the presiding authority of chief constables, men from various ministries, water bosses, generals and in one case a rear-admiral.

The negative reports were filtered through to Downing Street where the Prime Minister was maintaining a personal round-the-clock vigil. Rowland Mayes had urged her to rest but she would have none of that.

'I'm perfectly all right, Roly.'

'You may need to—'

'I said, I'm *perfectly all right*, Roly. It's my *duty* to remain at my post. I expect others to, and I can't make an exception for myself.'

The Foreign Secretary gave in, subsiding into gloom. He believed Mrs Heffer was blaming him for the whole thing, seeing it as his responsibility to arrest Logan, and to get Hedge and Shard back. Shard anyway; the Prime Minister was still content to leave Hedge wherever he might be, which was presumably East Germany still—no-one had informed the FO differently, no-one had claimed Hedge. (By no-one the Foreign Secretary understood Moscow, the only other Power likely to be interested.) Mrs Heffer, earlier on, had enquired somewhat perfunctorily as to what lay in Hedge's head that might be extracted by a potential enemy. The Foreign Secretary had replied truthfully: nothing whatsoever. The facts about Logan/Schreuder were not exactly secret by this time.

They awaited news from the water fronts. Mrs Heffer paced the Cabinet Office, from which she was in constant touch, when required, with all the reservoirs and all the area headquarters. The telephones had not been silent: whenever Mrs Heffer had a brainwave she was on the line at once, propounding it. The area chiefs were of course polite and deferential each time, but there were audible sighs when the telephone was put down. Mrs Heffer didn't really know very much about water, about reservoirs, about plastic bags or about the deployment to best advantage of the available manpower.

Naturally enough there were false alarms: catches that caused excitement and were reported along the line before they had been properly checked out.

Mrs Heffer became impatient and angry.

'Old clothes in bags, things containing cartons from Macdonald's...some *unmentionable* things...fishermen's *picnic lunches* in cellophane. There's a lot of *sheer inefficiency* around these days, Roly.'

'Yes, Prime Minister.'

'Why is it?'

'I really don't know, Prime Minister. Of course, all this...it's most unusual.'

'What is?'

'Well—botulin, Prime Minister.'

Mrs Heffer snorted. 'Botulin may be. Doing a job properly is *not*. Or shouldn't be. People in *responsible positions* are supposed to use their initiative. Not make silly reports.'

'I agree, Prime Minister.'

When two more such false alarms were reported, Mrs Heffer hooted angrily into the telephone. Her comments were made known at the headquarters nationwide and for a long time no reports at all came in, which made her very restless. Rowland Mayes took the brunt of her restlessness, and began to squirm in his seat. It was all so terribly unfair, he thought. He had always been a loyal Hefferite, admiring her very greatly indeed, but now he was having his doubts. She was something of a tartar and he had a sensitive mind. But of course he could appreciate her dreadful anxieties. Tetchiness was perhaps natural enough. If only somebody would find Logan; why, all the police forces in the Western continent were looking for him! He must be somewhere, surely? But then finding Logan was not of itself enough: found, he had yet to be conceded to. Or else.

Rowland Mayes, as Mrs Heffer went on with her nagging, gave a tactful cough and interrupted. Really, he'd had enough. He said deferentially, 'Prime Minister, I think perhaps I'd better return to the FO.'

'Why, Roly?'

Not the truth, that would never do. 'Well, Prime Minister...so as to keep more in touch—'

'There is a telephone.'

'Yes, there is, of course. But to have my finger actually on the—'

'Rubbish, Roly, you wouldn't make the *very slightest* difference. Your place, your *duty*, is here. This is a Foreign Office matter. Or very largely it is. Besides...I need you. You're a comforting influence.'

The Foreign Secretary gaped. Mrs Heffer

had never, ever, softened before. He simply couldn't understand it, but he smiled and blushed; he had been paid the most tremendous and signal compliment, a real tribute, and he was immensely pleased. He didn't know what to say; and while he was thinking of something suitable and grateful, the telephone rang again and Mrs Heffer answered. A plastic-type bag had been found in the Siblyback reservoir in the West Country—in Cornwall, not far from Liskeard. Carefully opened and its contents analysed, it had been confirmed as containing botulin spores.

'What action, Prime Minister—'

'I shall ring the Palace first,' Mrs Heffer announced.

The room was indeed comfortable. A big bed, a four-poster with curtains...Hedge could imagine a princess of the Russian royal house having slept in it. That bed could have been witness to many things in its time. The promised desk was a really splendid roll-top bureau of some expensive wood inlaid with what looked like real gold. The carpet was Chinese, and thick, very easy on the feet. There was a big window with a view over the Kremlin walls and a square beyond, and many tall buildings with domes and cupolas bathed in sunlight that had at last broken through the snow. That sunlight gave a promise, a heartening promise of better things, of God having penetrated the steely core of atheism with His sunbeams. There were, admittedly, bars over the window on the outside, but Hedge allowed this as being perfectly natural since he might be thought of as a possible escapee and never mind the great distance to ground level...leaning close to the window, he saw a roof not far beneath, and other roofs adjacent. Yes, a perfectly proper precaution. In the circumstances.

The chamber pot in a gilded cupboard beside the great bed was empty. Clean, too. The Russians were more civilised than the East Germans.

There was an old-fashioned bell-pull, an affair of heavy velvet with a tassel. Hedge wondered what would happen if he pulled it: room service? With all the luxury around, it might well be. He didn't pull it, but sat in a vast armchair before the flickering flames of a recently-lit coal fire. He cudgelled his brains for something to tell the Russian Foreign Minister out of

261

his virtually non-existent store of relevant knowledge. "Comfortable custody" was very comfortable indeed; he must not risk losing it for the other thing. But what in God's name was he to say that would be appreciated as helpful to the wretched Russians? With luck, something would come. He must not lose heart. He was, after all, on the fringe of diplomacy. Like all diplomats, he should be able to dissemble a little. Suddenly, he thought of Shard. Shard, with his policeman's mind, would call it waffle.

Hedge eyed the bell-pull again. The Foreign Minister, or had it been the gaunt man with the evil face, had promised books. There were no books; Hedge believed that if he read something, depending of course on what it was, but something relevant, then ideas might come. Or they might not...he didn't agitate the bell-pull. He wished to avoid being a nuisance. As it happened, a few minutes later the door was unlocked and a young woman stood there, looking at him guardedly.

He had been promised a woman.

This must be her. She addressed him in English. 'Hedge.'

'Yes. Er...' Hedge got to his feet.

'I come in, please.'

'Yes. Er...'

She came in, shutting the door behind her. Also locking it; the key was deposited in accordance with tradition down her décolletage. Hedge swallowed; she was bony, very angular, with flattish hair—dank, Hedge would have called it if asked. She had a sour smell, rancid, like butter that had gone off, such as would have been rejected by Mrs Millington. Yet there was an attraction undoubtedly. Hedge swallowed again. 'Er...'

She seemed to understand his dilemma. She moved closer, baring her teeth, spreading the rancidity around like a cloak. She said, 'I am here for your pleasure. You understand?'

'Yes,' he said, clearing his throat. 'I—I think I do, yes.' He felt a tremendous throbbing of his heart. He had been much disappointed by the wretched young woman from the taxi in Berlin—disappointed in retrospect, since his sudden projection into the back of the sugar-beet lorry had left him no time for his mental processes just then. Now, presumably, there would be no such interruptions.

He licked his lips; they had gone very

dry. He felt suddenly dried up all over.

Shard had found no lorry, no suitable lorry in which to stow away, during his prowl around the meaner streets behind the stores. After that he had walked on, closer to the Brandenburg Gate. Some way short of it the traffic was halted, waiting in queue for entry. As Shard watched, a big car carrying CD plates came up from behind, nosing past the line of traffic: preferential treatment. The registration was West German. Taking a chance, Shard moved out into the roadway, in front of the big car, waving it down. The chauffeur spoke through his wound-down window. Shard ignored him, tapped on the glass of the rear compartment, where two men and a woman sat in conversation. The chauffeur got out and closed in behind, but the man nearest Shard reached out and lowered his window a little way. In German he asked what was going on.

Shard said, 'Logan. Or Schreuder. I think you know who I mean.' Logan was big news now, Logan and his threat.

'You are not Logan?'

Briefly, Shard grinned. 'Not old enough.' The chauffeur, standing behind him, was ready for trouble. 'Detective Chief Superintendent Shard of the British Foreign Office. I have to get through to my embassy soonest possible. I'd be glad of any assistance. I have no documentation.'

There was a conversation that Shard couldn't catch. Then the diplomat opened the door. 'Get in,' he said. 'If you are an impostor, you will be dealt with.'

The chauffeur was nodded back to his seat and Shard got in. He thanked the diplomat. 'I'm no imposter, believe me. But I realise I don't look the part of a British copper. What will the reaction at the cross-over point be?'

The diplomat spoke to the chauffeur through a rubber tube. The car started up, moved on for the entry. 'There will be no trouble,' he said.

He was right; there was no trouble. The CD plates saw to that. The car was waved through and the guard saluted. Minutes later Shard was into the Western Sector. The car dropped him at the Consulate-General. He was accompanied into the building by the man who had done the talking; there was a wait before he was questioned by an official and passed. The German diplomat went away. Shard asked for the security line to Whitehall. On the way to it he asked about Hedge. In East German hands, he was told, so far as was known.

Rowland Mayes was still with the Prime Minister when the call came through from the Foreign Office. 'Shard's reported back, Prime Minister,' he said when the call was cut.

'Let us be thankful for that, Roly. Is there anything else—has Shard found anything out?'

'Logan is dead, Prime—'

'Dead? Good heavens, Roly, where does that leave us? Do we assume the threat's past, that—'

'No, Prime Minister, I'm afraid not. Another man comes into the picture. A man named Wolfgang Brosak. An old colleague of Logan's, an equally convinced and committed Nazi.'

Mrs Heffer tapped a pencil sharply on her blotting-pad. 'And?'

'And Brosak takes over from Logan. Lock, stock and barrel.'

'The threat remains, the botulin?'

'I'm afraid so, Prime Minister, yes. And of course the alternative, the result of

266

failure to concede.'

'And this Brosak? Where is he? Has Shard *got* him, Roly?'

'No, Prime Minister. He's searching for him. That's all we know at this moment.'

'Find out all that's known about this Brosak, Foreign Secretary, *at once.*'

'Yes, Prime Minister, that's being done already.' Rowland Mayes tried to conceal an involuntary sigh. The omens were poor: when Mrs Heffer was angry with him she always addressed him as Foreign Secretary. Fury made her formal. And once again she was casting the blame on him, her handy whipping boy.

The young woman had left. Before doing so, somewhat angrily, she opened a bag she had been carrying on entry and which she had deposited on the top of the bureau.

'As also promised,' she said, 'the book.'

'Book?'

'Book, yes. With the compliments of Comrade Voss.' She laid the book down. It was a biography of Kim Philby. 'Enjoy it, please.'

She left the room, locking Hedge in once again. He sat down with a thump in the comfortable chair, his mind rioting around in circles. He had rejected the woman's advances, not because he wanted to—quite the reverse—but because he had suddenly realised he was inadequate, not to put too fine a point on it, and also because he believed it might be dangerous and could lead to compromise and more threats of a personal nature this time. Photographs were still on his mind; the Russian outlook was tricky in the extreme, really diabolical, and it was perfectly possible that cameras were concealed in the woodwork or somewhere and that would never do. In the Foreign Office it was essential to have clean hands. Hedge, having remained clean now, comforted himself with the reflection that it was no doubt because of his worry over cameras and compromise that had led to his being inadequate...

But then a very nasty thought: the young woman having failed, the Russians might now send in the young man. Hedge did not believe much in Russian altruism; the young woman had tried to pump him—he'd sussed that out in no time. He'd been clever over that, giving nothing away, not that he had anything to give away, but they might try again, misinterpreting his desires and not believing his earlier reaction to the proposal of a young man.

Fearfully he awaited the next unlocking of the door.

When it came, it was only a meal. A very sumptuous meal, clear soup, very good soup, caviare...a bottle of an excellent Yugoslavian wine. Hedge, though his over-riding fear robbed him of his usual appetite, ate and drank; he had to keep his strength up; also, if possible, his spirits. Hunger led to depression, he knew that.

The Siblyback reservoir near Liskeard in Cornwall was now in the clear, according to government analysts. The bag had been intact; and it was considered unlikely that more than the one would have been deposited. There was enough botulin in the bag to have killed half the population of Great Britain. In Whitehall, spirits rose. If all the other bags could similarly be located and removed, the teeth of the threat would have been removed also. Rowland Mayes, however, uttered a word of warning, of more gloom.

'Logan had an organisation here, Prime Minister. We must expect Brosak to have the same—Shard made that point—'

'Well?'

'More bags, Prime Minister. Replacements.'

'If he gets to hear.'

'Yes...yes, that's true. And of course there's no reason why he should, I suppose—'

Mrs Heffer's voice snapped. 'There is *every* reason, Foreign Secretary. The man isn't likely to be a complete fool, he'll have people watching and reporting. When I said if he gets to hear, I meant he's *not to be allowed* to get to hear, don't you understand?'

'I'm awfully sorry, Prime Minister, I—'

Mrs Heffer shushed Rowland Mayes with a gesture and seized the telephone. She spoke to the Home Office. 'This is the Prime Minister speaking. This is most urgent. The watch at the reservoirs *including Siblyback* is still to be *continuously alert* for any persons in the vicinity. Any such persons *lurking about* are to arrested *immediately*. I trust that is in fact already being done, but I wish to *reinforce it*. All reservoirs, yes, of course, what an utterly stupid question, Under-Secretary. And another thing: *full secrecy* is to be observed in regard to any bags found. Word is *certainly not* to reach the press, is that *quite clear?* Good.'

Mrs Heffer rang off, a glint in her eye. So many fools, it was very trying, very frustrating. Rowland Mayes, for one, was really no longer up to his job, he was basically an old woman who had been found out by botulin.

Ten minutes later another of the security lines rang. It was Scotland Yard. Another bag had been found, this time in the Ladybower reservoir in the Peak District, not far from Sheffield. 'Good,' Mrs Heffer said into the telephone.

'Not good, Prime Minister. The bag was burst. We think it got snagged on some fisherman's gear. We—'

'So the reservoir is contaminated?'

'It must be regarded as so, yes.'

Mrs Heffer became very brisk. 'Warnings,' she said. 'All places, all homes, all hospitals and so on—everywhere that's on the Ladybower supply. No taps to be turned on, no water used. At this moment, not even *boiled* water. Police cars to go round with loud-hailers. Warnings to be broadcast on the local radio station.' She rang off. At the other end of the line, the Commissioner sighed. What a woman. All that had been ordered already.

Mrs Heffer had turned on Rowland Mayes. Before she spoke he came up with a piece of information. 'Ladybower,' he said ruminatively. 'Forty years ago...they submerged the little village of Ashopton, didn't they...? It holds ten thousand million gallons of water, Prime Minister—'

'For heaven's sake, Foreign Secretary, if you can't be *useful*, shut up.'

Now it was night over Berlin. Shard had spent the day partly in going over the blown-up microfilm files on Wolfgang Brosak, faxed across from Whitehall, partly in carrying out a daytime recce of the Western sector. He was not over familiar with Berlin and a lot of rebuilding had taken place since the last time a job had brought him here. Moving about the streets, keeping an eye watchful for Brosak but recognising the needles-in-a-haystack element, he thought about the Whitehall files. Brosak, a one-time Hitler Youth and then a member of the SS, was on record as an associate of known war criminals. He had been involved in any number of neo-Nazi activities in the years after the war. Other things too: a natural thug, a born terrorist, he had become involved with the

IRA and the Bader-Meinhoff gang. He was believed to be behind many killings, many bomb explosions, including a number that had involved children. In one of these, thirty-two schoolchildren on a coach outing had been smashed to pieces when a bridge over a deep valley had been blown up. But nothing had ever been pinned on him. He'd been much too careful, much too fly for the security services. Always cover: alibis and so on, unbreakable; just a dedicated scientist, working away in his laboratory under the noses of the British Army of the Rhine.

In the files there had been photographs. Wolfgang Brosak at neo-Nazi rallies, Wolfgang Brosak in Hitler-style uniform, with swastikas and jackboots, giving the Nazi salute as he heiled the memory of his Führer. *Deutschland Über Alles,* and all that, glorying in what he had been told of the great days of the 'thirties—told, no doubt, by Logan/Schreuder among others. Seeing the leaders of the Third Reich in cars following the splendid armies marching along Unter den Linden and beneath the Brandenburg Gate into the Thiergarten for Herr Hitler to address them in his uplifting tones. Hitler, Goering, Goebbels and the rest, including even the venerable old man von Hindenburg, who had come out in support of Hitler years before to become the President of the German Reich that would last, so Hitler had said, for a thousand years. Shard knew that the old German officer class, the Prussian landowners with their long record of military prowess tempered with chivalry had despised von Hindenburg for that betrayal, as they had despised the Führer and all his sycophants of the so-called elite SS.

Night now; and the beer cellars and bars and drinking clubs filled with people and streaming out light when the doors were opened. Pools of light on the pavement, dappling the snow. That snow was lying thickly underfoot and more was still coming down, and there was a wind. It was a bitter night, not one for walking the streets, and there were in fact few people about, those that were either looking as though they were bound for some night work, shift work, or poor and thinly clad with no homes to go to. Every big city of the world had its homeless, the no-hopers who night after weary, chilling night slept rough and got their sustenance from the dustbins of the smart restaurants and hotels, or from the soup kitchens provided by the various charitable organisations.

Shard drifted, openly. It was the quickest way, or could be—the only way now, for time was desperately short if Brosak knew Logan was dead. And it was possible he did; he had those contacts inside the Democratic Republic. If Logan's body had been found, the word would leak to those whose business it was to keep ears to the ground and eyes to keyholes.

It was at 2 a.m the next day that Hedge in Moscow was taken from his "comfortable custody" and marched under escort out from the Foreign Ministry into the cruel snow, and into the grim buildings of the Lubyanka Prison.

14

All the districts supplied from the Lady-bower reservoir were now without water. There were two other reservoirs in the complex—Howden and Derwent—and these were so far uncontaminated. Efforts were being made to bring clean water in tankers to the distressed areas, with particular reference to hospitals and such places. By now there was considerable anxiety nationwide. Already there had been a rush on the supermarkets for bottled water of various kinds, any kind would do, and now the shelves were empty.

There was no further report of burst botulin bags but the worry had gone deep. The whole country was now expectant of having no water in the taps at any moment. Life would change drastically; there wouldn't even be standpipes, of course. In conditions where no-one washed, other diseases could spread, in the cities especially, and no-one would ever feel clean again; danger from lice and fleas could lurk in every brush-past in a train, a bus, a shop. The Prime Minister was not unaware of all this. She had conferred closely and lengthily with the officials of the Health Ministry, who were themselves in some disarray, not knowing what could be done about it if all the other botulin bags reached the limit of their water-resistance and burst. Nothing to compare with this had ever happened before.

'Not even during the war,' the Ministry's Chief Medical Officer said. 'The Germans could have used botulin against our reservoirs, but they never did.'

'No. And why?' Mrs Heffer demanded. 'Because they knew we would have *retaliated.*' She heaved her breasts up, stiffly, straightening her backbone. 'But this time we can't retaliate. We're absolutely *caught.* As we all know, there's just the one way out offered by these *abominable* people.'

'War with—' Rowland Mayes began but was cut short.

'That's not even *mentionable,* Foreign Secretary. It would be *utterly improper* and not even to be thought about.' Her face said other things: that she was thinking very hard about it and would have liked nothing better than to topple communism finally from its throne and never mind winds of change blowing out of Russia. But she knew the electorate... She went on with a touch of venom, 'Which leaves us with your people, Foreign Secretary.'

'Hedge and Shard? Yes.'

'Unless you have anything better to offer.'

Rowland Mayes adjusted his owl-like glasses and examined some notes he had made on a sheet of paper. Looking up a moment later he said, 'America, Prime Minister.'

Mrs Heffer was impatient. 'As you *know*, or should know, I've had no assistance *whatsoever* from America, so—'

'Ah—no warlike assistance, I agree. I had something else in mind, Prime Minister.'

'Well?'

'Water, Prime Minister. From America, in those giant tankers. Across the Atlantic, you know...as a humanitarian gesture, they'd surely not deny us that at such a time...would they?'

Mrs Heffer gasped audibly, then spoke as if to a lunatic. 'I have no idea and I've no intention of finding out. My dear Foreign Secretary...have you *no conception at all* of how *long* it would take your precious tankers to cross the Atlantic? They're not *jet aircraft*. And have you any conception at all of what a *fleabite* all their combined cargoes would be to the population...the population of the *whole of Great Britain?* Have you?'

Rowland Mayes had gone a deep red; he shifted very uncomfortably in his seat. 'I'm sorry, Prime Minister.'

'Have you?' Mrs Heffer pressed. When she asked a question she expected, not an apology, but an answer.

'Have I—?' Rowland Mayes looked puzzled.

'God give me strength,' Mrs Heffer said, ostentatiously lifting her eyes to the ceiling. *'Any conception?'*

'Er...no, Prime Minister. Not really.'

Mrs Heffer's eyes flashed the war alternative. The future looked extremely bleak. The whole country faced death. Such a statement might seem alarmist, might seem even ludicrously melodramatic. But it was the stark truth. And Mrs Heffer knew that everything was set to go if it became necessary. Leaving no stones unturned, as was her way, she had seen to that, just as a precaution, of course... No-one in the whole country, no-one anywhere else except for the Cabinet and Defence Ministry and the brass of NATO, knew that for sure. Mrs Heffer was astonished in fact that the President of the United States, who would certainly have been kept informed by his Secretary of State—for the US supremo in West Germany would have reported—hadn't been on the line already. And talk of the devil, a half-minute later he was.

He was in something of a state. 'Hey, look, Charlotte. What's all this about readiness?'

'You know very well, George. You know what we in this country are facing. This *diabolical* threat.' Mrs Heffer's fingers were clenching and unclenching around a lace handkerchief and her face was formidable as she felt the emanation of American stubbornness and insularity. Just, as she'd remarked earlier in Cabinet, like last time and the time before. 'You *know perfectly well*, we face *extinction!* Total extinction, total slaughter of all our people. That, we *simply cannot face*, George. Really, you *must* see that.'

'Uh-huh. I'm sorry to hear this, Charlotte, very sorry.' There was a pause; Mrs Heffer waited, her heart thudding behind her breasts, rising to her mouth as it seemed. 'Do I take it you're asking for our support?'

'Of course I am, George,' Mrs Heffer snapped.

'I see. Well, now. It goes without saying that you have our moral support—'

'I'm not interested in moral—'

'After all, so many of us have our roots in England and Scotland. Ireland, too. We have one hell of a lot in common, Charlotte, right?'

'Yes—'

'And there's the special understanding—'

'Of course, George. Our two nations—each must back the other, I'm sure you agree.'

'Yes, sure. Mind, the special understanding... maybe not so sure as it was with Ronald and Maggie, I don't know. But sure, you have our support. But no war, right?'

Mrs Heffer's body stiffened rigidly, then she began to shake with rage. 'You mean you *won't* support us, Mr President?'

'Why no, I didn't say that. I said I would. Short of war. Only maniacs go to war, these days—'

'Thank you for your honesty, Mr

President. In that case I shall have to go it alone.' Mrs Heffer banged the receiver down. She faced her ministers angrily. Seething, in fact. *'Lily-livered,'* she said. *'Gutless!* Afraid, I suppose, to face Congress.'

They all knew precisely what she was referring to even though the word "war" had not been mentioned from the Downing Street end. Rowland Mayes, basically a brave man and with an obstinacy of his own, chanced his arm. He gave an embarrassed cough and said, 'The election, Prime Minister, our British election—'

'What about it?'

'Well, Prime Minister—if we attack the Soviet—'

'The electors will vote for the Green Party, is that what you're saying?'

'Well, not necessarily the—'

'My dear Foreign Secretary, what a *stupid* fool you are. If the botulin does what this man Brosak threatens, there *won't be any electors.* They'll all be *dead!'*

As Hedge had feared, it was Dresden all over again. Also as he had feared, it was much worse. *Glasnost* and *perestroika,* whichever was which, had not lightened the terrible aura of the Lubyanka. The very walls were bloodstained in Hedge's imagination and his ears seemed to hear the dreadful cries of the afflicted, the tortured millions who had passed this way but once, en route for the Siberian salt mines and labour camps, or death. He had been taken, not yet to a cell, but to what was clearly an interrogation chamber with thick stone walls and the gaunt man seated invisible but vocal behind a light the very bright beam of which was shining straight into Hedge's eyes. Behind him were two armed guards, one of them a woman, which Hedge didn't like at all; it was infra dig for a woman to watch a man's humiliation, or rather for a man to be humiliated in front of a woman, and he was certain this was what was going to happen.

For a long time the gaunt man didn't utter. That, Hedge knew, was all part of it, part of the build-up, the induction of anxiety, of terror. In the end it was Hedge himself who broke the silence.

'Why have I been moved?' he asked.

'You were comfortable, Hedge?'

'Yes, I was. I thought that was the idea. Comfortable custody.'

'It is not the idea now.'

'Oh.'

'You have not signified that you will speak. That you will tell us what we wish to know.'

'Yes, I see. So—'

'So unless now you talk, then the uncomfortable custody. Have you read the biography of Comrade Philby?'

This was an unexpected question. Hedge answered truthfully. 'I'm afraid not, but I did appreciate the loan of it.'

'Yes. It is of no consequence.' Kim Philby was dismissed from further consideration, but Hedge was left to wonder why he had been mentioned in the first place. Unless, of course, it was a kind of hint, a suggestion that those who threw in their lot with the Soviet Union would become honoured, well treated, given a luxurious flat near the Kremlin, live off the somewhat thin fat of the land, end up as heroes. Hedge had no wish to remain in Russia; he couldn't wait to get back to London, his one over-riding concern being that he might never get back if he didn't play his cards right.

He had no cards to play.

The gaunt man began an exposition of

what uncomfortable custody was going to be like. He described the smallness of the cell to be occupied by Hedge; there would be space to stand up and to sit, but not to lie down. There would be no window and the electric light would of course be constant. The celing would be low, the air unfresh. He would be brought out for interrogation like now, and this would happen at odd times and, until he spoke, frequently. He would not be allowed to sleep. Through a spyhole a guard would watch, and whenever he was seen to nod off he would be awoken with a loud noise or a sharp prod. The food would be scanty and unpalatable, enough to sustain life and that was all. There might be persuasion of a very unpleasant kind.

Hedge shook, tried to conceal the shake that racked his whole body. He said in a high voice, 'This is all most irregular and again I demand—ask, I'm sorry—to see the British Ambassador. It's my right. I'm an important person in Whitehall, you realise. My Prime Minister will react most strongly if I'm harmed.'

'Pish.'

'I beg your pardon?'

'Your Prime Minister has not reacted at all.'

The wind gushed from Hedge's sails. He gasped, then said, 'Well, that's simply because she doesn't know I'm here, isn't it? If you haven't reported—'

'It is known that she knew you were in East German hands, in Dresden. She did not react.'

'Oh.' Hedge felt quite desperate now. It was too bad; he was being left, disowned by Whitehall, by Mrs Heffer whom he had always so strongly supported, a fine woman with all the right ideas. Or so he had thought. Now anger began to rise. He knew, of course, had always known, that persons were at times disowned by their governments in the interest of diplomacy and, it had to be admitted, expediency. But he had never envisaged that such would apply to himself, highly-placed as he was in the Foreign Office. Lesser people perhaps; not him. He could scarcely believe it; but he was forced to. The gaunt man must have spoken the truth. If Mrs Heffer had authorised any intervention, he wouldn't be where he was.

The gaunt man cruelly underlined the point. 'You have been abandoned by your female Prime Minister. You know, of course, the British saying.'

'Oh. Do I?'

'Yes. "The female of the species is more deadly than the male," Rudyard Kipling.'

'Ah. You read Kipling?'

'Yes.'

'So does Mrs Heffer, you know.'

'I did not know, Hedge. But do not let us discuss Rudyard Kipling now. Time is short. Look.'

The gaunt man reached out and pressed a switch. The interrogation chamber was at once flooded with light. Hedge looked about in horror, his flesh creeping with his terrible fear. On one wall a whip was looped around a rusty nail, a whip with many most dreadful-looking leather thongs. There were real bloodstains on floor and wall, nothing imaginary about them this time. On a table were instruments of diabolical torture—thumb-screws, spikes for possible insertion under finger-nails and toe-nails. There was an instrument like a clamp, an iron horror with big curved claws and a large divided handle; Hedge had once seen something like it in a shop window in Launceston in Cornwall—that had been a device for castrating bulls.

287

The gaunt man saw where his attention was so glassily fixed. 'To crush,' he said helpfully.

'Crush?'

'The testicles. The pain, I understand, is extreme. And afterwards the voice is high.'

Sweat poured down Hedge's face and neck, soaking into his filthy collar. What barbarians he was faced with; it was really quite appalling, far removed from the British way of doing things, indeed from all decency. Why, they even kept a man dirty in order to take away his confidence and self-esteem—even in comfortable custody he hadn't been accorded any clean linen. He closed his eyes against the other instruments of cruelty; he'd seen more than enough. He was aware of the man and woman behind him, the guards. He sensed that they wished torture to begin, that their mouths drooled with expectancy. The woman would probably wield the handle of the crusher.

'Well?' This was the gaunt man. 'You speak?'

'I—I don't know anything. I've already told you that.'

'Yes. But speak nevertheless.'

It sounded crazy, but Hedge knew that it wasn't. If you spoke, you often released things that helped the questioner, even when you didn't wish to release or help. That was the way things went. Secrets—or what the questioner wished to know—tended to come out. If you waffled, it would soon become apparent but it might not matter. Waffle for long enough, and the end result could come close to truth.

Hedge said hoarsely, 'You know just as much as I do. I really can't help.'

'Try, Hedge. Go over again what you know.'

More sweat ran. Hedge said, 'You know about Logan and his threat to Britain. There's nothing I can add to that, there really isn't. I've said so, to your Foreign Minister.'

'Yes.'

'Then why go on pressing me like this?' A note of hysteria was creeping in now, Hedge beginning to lose control. From behind the beam—the overall lighting having now been switched off again—he fancied he could make out a smile of satisfaction. He thought again about Mrs Heffer and her perfidy. Bitch, he thought, she's let me in for this...

The gaunt man spoke again, though not in answer to Hedge's question. He said, 'There is something you perhaps do not know about Logan. Something in fact that you cannot know, since you have been in custody. You wish to know, Hedge?'

Hedge nodded.

'Logan is dead,' the gaunt man said.

15

There had been some deaths. One, in Liskeard near the cleared Siblyback reservoir, was only peripherally connected with the threat. An elderly woman in a car, driving past the recreational area when the suspect bag was being brought ashore, had noticed a great fuss going on and had asked a policeman what it was all about. Apart from the fact of the bag's discovery, it had all been on TV and radio, but the elderly woman had become much agitated and after driving away had had a heart attack. The car had gone into the reservoir. Up near Sheffield, at the Ladybower reservoir, it had been a great deal more serious. Mrs Heffer's warnings by broadcast and police car had not been so swift as had the botulin. Before the pumping stations could be put out of action, before all the taps had been turned off, the botulin had arrived in the area served by Ladybower. A number of people had drunk the water or used it in other ways, and once the warnings had got through to them they immediately exhibited symptoms. The local doctors, and the casualty departments at the hospitals, became very busy.

Mrs Heffer was of course informed. She was much upset and said so. 'Those *poor* people. I take it everything is being done that can be done?'

'Yes, Prime Minister.'

'Good. Has this wretched disease been *actually diagnosed?*'

'Not yet, Prime Minister. It will take time for—'

'Yes, but we should surely assume they've *got it*, shouldn't we?'

'Yes—'

'That,' Mrs Heffer said with a long-suffering sigh, 'was what I meant by *diagnosed.*' She paused, frowned, leaned forward. 'Tell me, Doctor, are those brave men *at the sites* wearing gumboots or are they not?'

The Chief Medical Officer looked surprised. 'I really don't know, Prime Minister, but—'

'Then *find out*, if you please. Personal protection is *very important*. And rubber gloves.'

'Yes, Prime Minister, but botulin doesn't

enter the body through the feet.'

'One simply can't be too careful, can one?' Mrs Heffer said with finality.

Later the reports of the confirmed diagnoses came in. Not long after that, in some cases—chiefly the elderly or the already sick—the deaths. Mrs Heffer's salt cure did not seem to have worked.

In West Berlin that evening, Shard had had some initial luck, but the luck had turned sour on him. He had gone into a beer cellar on spec, still making himself obvious to anyone who might have reason to wish to contact him. He'd not had much hope, really. But that was just when luck had appeared to smile.

The beer cellar, a smoky place, not well lit, had been crowded to capacity with both East and West Germans, the former distinguishable by their less than prosperous look—men and women, Shard guessed, who had come over from the Democratic Republic to enjoy the fleshpots of the West for a brief evening out. Pushing through the press of bodies towards the bar, Shard had trodden on someone's toe when he had stepped backwards suddenly under pressure from a large bottom clad, despite the weather, in leather shorts.

He turned to apologise.

He came face to face with a young woman: Gerda Schmidt; Logan/Schreuder's grand-daughter who had given him the name and laboratory address of Wolfgang Brosak. And who had informed Brosak subsequently that he was on his way to Rinteln. That time, he had fallen into the trap. But now she was, once again, the one and only link he had with Brosak.

She was looking at him fearfully, eyes narrowed, breathing fast, a hunted look on her face. But she might not be aware that Shard knew she had led him into that Rinteln trap. Just might not. He took hold of her arm.

He said, 'You and I have things to talk about, Fräulein Schmidt.' He looked around; there was a table being vacated in a dark corner not far away. He pushed the girl towards it, nabbed it just in time.

So Logan was dead. Or was said to be.

Hedge was filled with elation, wanting desperately to believe what the gaunt man had said. With Logan dead, an enormous weight would be lifted from his shoulders and possibly the threat from those evil kidnappers in London would be negatived. Licking at dry lips he asked, 'How do you know he's dead?'

'We know,' the gaunt man answered in a flat tone. 'We know, which is enough for you, Hedge.'

'Yes, well...how do I know you're telling me the truth?'

'You do not know. You cannot know. All you have to do is to trust. Do you trust, Hedge?'

'I suppose so,' Hedge answered gloomily. Really, the man could be the most consummate liar, most Russians were, indeed most foreigners were, they didn't appear to see anything wrong in it.

'So now you know that Logan is dead.'

'Yes.'

There was a pause. 'Of this news you are glad.' It wasn't a question; it was a statement. But, in a sense, Hedge answered it.

He said, 'I never knew him personally, of course. But of course, since he's dead...it alters things.'

'It alters things, yes. But I say this—Logan you knew personally. This we know. You ask how we know. I answer that while you were in comfortable custody we were in touch with certain persons in your Foreign Office in London—'

'*Spies?*'

'Not spies. Agents.'

'Yes, I see.' Better not to make enemies at this stage: better not to argue. Uncomfortable custody loomed too close. 'What did these agents have to say?'

'That you were known to have had contacts with Logan/Schreuder many years ago. That you knew him personally.'

'Ah. Well, yes—I'd forgotten, as a matter of fact.'

'You had not forgotten, Hedge. Other persons of prominence in London also had personal contacts. Personal contacts are always suspect. You will agree?'

There was something very nasty and suggestive in the gaunt man's tone. Hedge said, 'Perhaps you will tell me...what exactly you're getting at? Talking like that about personal contact, you see?'

'Not buggery.'

'Not?'

'Not. Although it may have taken place.'

'It most certainly did not!'

'Perhaps. But do not let us become embroiled in buggery. I speak of other things. Of bribery. Of favours given.' There was a pause from behind the bright light. 'Not sexual favours. Logan, as I have said, is dead. From him you are now safe. So are the other London persons. That is why you are glad to hear that Logan is dead. Glad also will be the other London persons. You agree?'

Slowly, knowing there was more behind this than met the eye, more than had yet met the ear, Hedge nodded.

'Then I think you will see your way clear, Hedge. Logan is dead. Us, and our agents in your Foreign Office, are not dead. Do you understand?'

Hedge felt sick, sick and desperate. He began to shake again. It was all so unfair. Out of the frying-pan...and it was all Mrs Heffer's fault. If only she had rescued him, insisted in her customary blunt fashion that the Russians release him immediately. He felt absolutely no loyalty now, none whatsoever. The home authorities had asked for it. He would play ball with the Russians now. After all, Kim Philby had and look where that had got him (not London, certainly, but London would be dross to a dishonoured man, and would be likely to mean only Pentonville when things came out via Moscow).

'All right, then,' he said with a touch of vengefulness. 'I have a few things to say after all.'

In the beer cellar Shard asked probing questions. The girl's unease increased when Shard revealed that he knew she had informed on him to Brosak. At first she denied it; then said she had been under pressure. That might or might not have been true. But Shard didn't press: it was no longer important. She didn't know, or said she didn't know, that her grandfather was dead. Shard found no reason to doubt her. She showed shock, she showed emotion. Both feelings seemed to Shard quite genuine. She wanted to know the details; Shard told her honestly.

'So,' she said, 'you were the last person to see my grandfather alive?'

He nodded. Her face was pale, more pinched than ever. He said, 'I'm sorry. About your grandfather. Because he was your grandfather and you were fond of him.' He added, 'Brosak was initially responsible for his death. I did my best for him. I didn't want him to die.'

'No. You had been looking for him, I know that, of course.'

'He was wanted in England, Fräulein. Now there is someone else who is wanted.'

'In England?'

'Yes. Your grandfather's old friend. Wolfgang Brosak.' He paused, searching her face. 'Last time we met, I gathered you didn't approve of all the raking up of old loyalties and old enmities. That might have been an act and probably was. But you sounded convincing...when you said you preferred to let Adolf Hitler remain dead—'

'Yes,' she said. 'I do not like all that, the senseless recreating of what is past.'

'What is best forgotten. I believe you may have...done what you did—informing Brosak about me—out of a sense of loyalty to your grandfather. Rather that than simply to help Brosak.'

She was looking at him closely; no-one seemed interested in them; the drinkers moved past their table without a second glance. Singing started, nothing neo-Nazi. They were all just happy that East and West were together, that the end had come for hostility with the shattering a year or so before of the Berlin Wall. Gerda Schmidt asked, 'Why is Brosak so much wanted in England, Herr Shard?'

There was no reason why he shouldn't tell her the facts now. The German press—he had been told this in the Consulate-General—had reported what was likely to happen in the British Isles, largely copying the reports that had filled the London newspapers. Gerda Schmidt would have read the papers; but she quite likely didn't know that Wolfgang Brosak was behind all that.

He said quietly, 'You'll have read about the botulin.'

She nodded. 'Yes. So?'

'So it's all down to Brosak. And your grandfather. Now your grandfather's dead, you see, Brosak has taken over. Brosak's the brains, Brosak's the scientist. And I've every reason to believe he can kill everyone in Britain if he puts his mind to it. Which he's going to do...any time now.'

The girl sat in silence. Her face was paler than ever and Shard detected a shake in her fingers. Unless she was a good actress, she had been shaken by what she had heard. She said after a while, 'Wolfgang Brosak. I know where he is. But tell me this, Herr Shard: the threat of the botulin. There is an "unless", is there not?'

'Yes. Unless the British government

mounts a strike against the Soviet Union, Brosak releases his botulin. It's vital for world peace that he's taken before either of those things happen.'

She shook her head in what looked like wonder. She said, 'You told me you believed Brosak would do—what he has threatened. Do you believe your country will respond with war?'

Shard lifted his hands palms upward. 'I pray to God not. On the other hand...'

'On the other hand, there will be much death in Britain.'

'That's right. Also, there's yet another hand.'

'How, another hand?'

He gave a hard, grim laugh. 'Not how, but who. Mrs Heffer.'

She seemed to understand. She stood up. She said, 'Come. I will show you where Wolfgang Brosak is.'

He thanked her; they left the beer cellar, going out into the bitterness of the snow, lying largely in slush but with more falling as though it would never stop. For certain reasons Shard was never to find out for sure whether or not Gerda Schmidt was a good actress, or whose side she was really on.

The orders had been finalised from Defence Ministry. Strike aircraft with missiles loaded had taken off from certain bases in Cumbria and Northumberland and Yorkshire. Also in Scotland. They awaited the final order, the order that could come only from the Prime Minister. The nuclear submarines with their stocks of intercontinental ballistic missiles were equally ready, deep in their sea stations from where they could strike right into the heart of the Soviet Union. Mrs Heffer had had a monumental row by telephone with the Supreme Commander of NATO, accusing him of being an American, an accusation that she had quickly altered to a typical American.

'That's what I am, ma'am. That's what I aim to stay. There will be no goddamn troop or armour movement in my command. Not unless it's authorised by my President. If you wish to go mad, ma'am, then you'll have to go mad via your navy and air force. You can count the USA out this time.'

Mrs Heffer had slammed down the telephone. Very well, she thought, if it does come to the pinch, we're ready. If we have to, we'll go it alone. In that moment she felt very Churchillian, very much the lone bulldog in a Union Jack jacket. Her heart swelling with emotion she left what she now regarded as her command HQ and went to her bedroom. Here she knelt by the side of the double bed and clasped her hands in prayer. God would of course defend the right but He had to be asked decently first; also perhaps briefed by the woman on the spot, He being not exactly on the spot and not, perhaps, seeing things in entirely the way she saw them, which was natural enough. So she told God about the botulin, and the suffering that would come; she told Him about the stupid recalcitrance of the Americans who didn't want to get involved. She told Him her views of the Russians, that really the world would be a safer place...she baulked at actually adding the words "without them" since that might be seen as presumptuous, it being, after all, *God's* world rather than hers. She told Him about Logan, now dead, and the fact that his death had not removed the terrible threat. She didn't mention Hedge or Shard, she having forgotten their names.

She told God what she intended to do and asked if that would be all right.

She waited for an answer; none came that she could identify. Now she was really on her own. But she would go the whole hog. Rowland Mayes would make a fuss, so would all, or most, of the others. But she would prevail. She would *not* allow millions of Britains to be slaughtered by a *bug*. And the Americans could stew in their own juice.

Mrs Heffer, jaw out-thrust, returned to her HQ.

'I believe,' Hedge said, speaking now to the Foreign Minister in the Kremlin, around which it was still snowing, 'that my Prime Minister is thinking of mounting a strike against the Soviet Union.'

'Yes. We know this. We have already said so to you.'

'Oh. Yes—yes, you have.' Hedge, after his dreadful experience in the interrogation chamber in the Lubyanka, was upset and more than a little bewildered. He was now forced to embroider. Just a little, not much: he knew Mrs Heffer's wilful and determined character and knew she had no time for communism wherever and in whatever guise (*glasnost* or *perestroika*) it might lurk. He could make a good guess. He said, 'I happen to know she *intends* to mount this strike. Positively.'

'Positively. She has entrusted you with this information.'

Hedge took a chance and a deep breath. 'Yes.'

'Then you are of very much importance?'

'Some might say so, yes.'

'Of more importance than at first we thought. I wonder why your Prime Minister has made no representation on your behalf.'

'Ah. Possibly,' Hedge said, half believing this himself, or wishing to believe it, 'because you might have thought I...knew more than I did. If you follow?'

'But you do know more—you say.'

'Yes. Oh, yes.'

'Then how is this, Hedge?'

Hedge dithered. 'Mrs Heffer doesn't know everything though she may think she does. And talking about knowing...I'm surprised, if I may say so, that your agents in the British Foreign Office have not kept you better informed of Mrs Heffer's intentions.'

'We have no agents in the British Foreign

Office,' T M Voss said calmly.

Hedge indicated the gaunt man, present once again. 'He said you had.'

T M Voss waved a hand dismissively. 'It is of no matter. Of course we have our intelligences, all countries have, yours included. And of course we know of your Madame Heffer's intentions. This we know without you.'

'Oh.'

'Unless you have anything else to say, you are superfluous.'

'You mean—'

The Foreign Minister leaned forward, his face hard and threatening. 'You know well what I mean. The Lubyanka prison. And pressure—much pressure. We know what your function is in your Foreign Office, that you are very high up in security—and—'

'Not so very high up.' The squeak had returned to Hedge's voice. 'I'm certainly not the repository of all things secret, you must understand that. I'm very willing to help where I can, but...well, I may not be all that much help. If I can't be, I'm sorry.'

T M Voss appeared to lose patience. He made a gesture to the armed guards and

Hedge was seized and turned about with rough hands and marched away.

Foreign Minister T M Voss was reporting to the Chairman of the Presidium of the Supreme Soviet.

'The man Hedge.'

'Yes?'

'He is valueless, Comrade President. He is a woolly-minded idiot. This, Madame Heffer must know.'

'Presumably, yes, since she has not uttered to help him. Or he may perhaps be a plant?'

T M Voss shook his head firmly. 'I think not, Comrade President.'

'Yet he seems to wish to help us. He has revealed his country's intentions—oh yes, these we were aware of already. But now there seems a very clear certainty which our agents were unable to give us.'

'True, Comrade Chairman—'

'Has the man Hedge given us a time for the British attack?'

'No. I understand there is as yet no certainty as to the time, Comrade President. All hangs upon the man Brosak and his threat to the British reservoirs. Or rather, upon whether Madame Heffer concedes or does not concede. Until she had decided, we shall not know her time-table.'

'But we know Madame Heffer's mind. We know her character, her immense determination. What conclusion does that lead us to, Comrade Voss?'

'That she will not concede?'

'Exactly.' The Chairman rose to his feet, then pressed a bell-push on his desk top. A secretary entered. The Chairman passed his orders: the Presidium and the Council of Ministers were to assemble in full session as soon as this could be arranged. The Defence Minister and the chiefs of the army, navy and air force were to attend. The matter, the Chairman said, was of the utmost urgency.

As the secretary left the room, a telephone burred on the Chairman's desk. He answered, monosyllabically; then put the instrument down and spoke to T M Voss.

'The man Brosak, the West German—he has been apprehended in Berlin and is on his way here by air.'

16

Gerda Schmidt had said it was not far to where Brosak would be found. A matter of perhaps half a kilometre.

'A taxi?' she suggested. The snow made for uncomfortable walking. Shard vetoed taxis; he wished for a more furtive arrival. The girl had told him Brosak was living in the flat of a friend, a woman, also one of the Hitler lovers. Shard had a sudden thought that the woman could have had a bearing on Gerda Schmidt's betrayal of Brosak: jealousy? Just a thought and most probably baseless. Brosak would be somewhat too old for Fräulein Schmidt...

They trudged through the snowstorm, collars pulled about their necks, through the remains of Christmas, the tatty, damp tinsel. The wind blew, tugged at them unmercifully. Shard slowed the pace when Gerda said the flat was not far, a hundred metres along the street they had just entered.

Shard felt for the automatic that he had

been provided with by the West German police at the request of an official of the Consulate-General. They were no more than a dozen metres from the entry to the flat, a first-floor one in a modern block, when there was a sudden disturbance. Two men appeared from a doorway in front of them and began walking briskly along the street. From the entry to Brosak's flat a man came out, looked briefly up and down the street, outlined in the headlights of the passing traffic. Suddenly he seemed to freeze, then reached into his clothing and pulled out a gun. In that instant Shard recognised him: Brosak. Brosak making a getaway? In the instant of recognition, Brosak fired. His aim was bad; the bullet took the front near-side tyre of a big car. The driver seemed to lose control in the slushy conditions, slewed sideways, mounted the pavement. Shard was conscious of the two men moving forward fast towards Brosak, and then the car had hit Gerda Schmidt, running her down and crunching her head into the pavement. As it hit the wall behind and slewed the other way, the back end took Shard and knocked him down flat and his head hit the pavement, hard.

Shard, coming round after a couple of minutes, left the scene before an ambulance and the police could arrive. He went fast for the Consulate-General and put through a call to London, to the Foreign Office security section. He spoke to his Detective Inspector.

'Shard. I've lost Brosak. I don't know for sure, but I believe he's been hooked away. Possibly by Soviet agents, I'm not sure. Yes, I'm all right. Is there any word of Hedge?'

'Nothing further, sir. Still in East German custody so far as I know. What are you going to do now, sir?'

'Try to locate Brosak again,' Shard said, and rang off. There wouldn't, in fact, be much hope. If Brosak was in the hands of Soviet operators, it would be a case of next stop Moscow. And it looked very much as though he, Shard, had muffed it, finally this time. He gave a bitter, self-deprecatory laugh. Now, it looked as if it might land in Hedge's lap—Hedge, last reported in the hands of the East German police, might be in Moscow by now. Hedge, in Moscow with Brosak...

No further reports of the findings of plastic bags reached Whitehall. By now the homes and hospitals and workplaces in the area served by the Ladybower reservoir were suffering enforced drought. So far as possible the other two reservoirs in the vicinity, Howden and Derwent, were helping out so the situation was not in fact too drastic. There had been a number of sufferers from botulism and most had either died already or were expected to do so shortly. The main concern in Whitehall was lest the botulism should spread, the bags reaching bursting point in all the other reservoirs.

That, and what Mrs Heffer intended to do next. There was little doubt in the minds of her ministers that she was suffering a bad dose of war fever.

'It's difficult to blame her,' the Home Secretary said *sotto voce*. Even though Mrs Heffer was not currently in the room she was known to have long ears and she disliked being criticised. 'It's a very desperate situation indeed, as we all know. I don't see how she can be expected just to sit back and take it.'

'A very desperate remedy,' Rowland Mayes said.

The Home Secretary shrugged. 'Desperate situations call for desperate remedies,' he announced as though he had just dreamed up something new in the way of comment. But he believed what he was saying. Charity, he had always thought, began at home. Of course, it would be hard on the Russians, but there it was. It might even seem to the rest of the world like a dirty trick, to hit a country when it was down—down in the sense of facing so much internal dissent, parts of the Soviet Union itself wishing to break away from Moscow's domination, and so on and so forth. But you simply had to put your own people first, which was something Mrs Heffer always did. She didn't, in fact, like foreigners at all and really you couldn't blame her. The Home Secretary remembered very vividly an advertising slogan from his boyhood in the 'thirties: British Is Best.

How very, very true that had been.

Hedge was sent for once again, was brought from his terrible sojourn in uncomfortable custody. He had suffered badly from being unable to lie down, from claustrophobia, and from sheer dread of what was to happen to him next. When the armed men came for him again, he fancied it could even be for his execution or transportation to Siberia. Death and exile were still to some extent rife in Russia; the Russians were not very Christian, he believed, in spite of an agreement in 1989 between the Pope and Comrade Gorbachev to restore freedom of worship. And they really didn't take much notice of world opinion. In any case if he, Hedge, was to be sacrificed, then not many people in all the world were going to have their sleep disturbed. He wasn't that important. Britain, these days, had ceased making a fuss about her nationals being taken hostage. These days, no gunboats were sent. The British—or should he say, distastefully, the European—passport was just a sick joke now.

Hedge shivered and shook his way under escort along the dreadful corridors of the Lubyanka, corridors with thick carpets to drown screams, down in the divided two-man lift, a most dreadfully confined space, out into the snow in his dirty clothing, and into the Foreign Ministry which was at least plush and comfortable if such mattered now.

Was he to hear his sentence?

Or was he—sudden happy thought—to be told that he had at last been claimed, or acknowledged, by Mrs Heffer? He dare not dwell too hopefully on that. He must not tempt fate.

He was taken into the room where he had earlier been questioned. The gaunt man, that seemingly inevitable man of evil, was there. So was T M Voss. So were two generals and an admiral.

So was Wolfgang Brosak.

Hedge had not previously met Brosak. What he saw was a square-headed man, a man with an unmistakable German look, a man who had quite obviously been subjected to manhandling and worse— torture, very likely. His clothing was badly rumpled and in places torn. There was blood on his face and his left arm hung in an unnatural position as though it had been broken and then left unattended. His lips were swollen and behind them there appeared to be no teeth. Both eyes were blackened and he seemed to be on the brink of collapse.

T M Voss spoke. 'This is Brosak.'

Hedge, about to say how d'you do,

nodded instead. He had understood Shard to be searching for Brosak, and where was Shard now? In Russian custody, too? Or swanning about like any other policeman in the free world, leaving his chief to face untold horrors in the hands of barbarians?

'Brosak has been questioned. About your botulin, Hedge.'

'Botulin,' Hedge repeated stupidly, not really registering.

They told him. He shook his head. 'Rabies,' he said. 'Not botulin.'

'Not so. Botulin. It is now known, there is no secret. In Britain, the populace is very frightened. Madame Heffer is enraged. As I have said, Brosak has been questioned. He has not spoken. Not fully. Soon he will, and you will be present to listen.'

Hedge offered no comment. He had been shaken by the implications of botulin; he'd been out of touch and things moved so fast these days. T M Voss proceeded to make something of a speech. It was, he said, incumbent upon the Soviet leadership to assist the West when the West appeared unable to help itself. 'We in the Soviet Union have no animosity towards your people. We wish only to help...to prevent the widespread death that is threatened

316

by the unrepentant Nazi Brosak. Do you understand, Hedge?'

'Yes. I think I do.'

'And what have you to say to it?'

'Well...nothing really. Just that I'm very glad.'

'I see. You realise, of course, that we do not wish for war. War must never come about again. We are willing to go to any lengths to prevent that.'

'Yes, I see that.' Hedge was still in a state of utter terror and was much more concerned to know what was in store for himself than with any considerations such as war, botulin or Brosak. But he felt he should show some sort of response to what was apparently a neighbourly act on the part of the Russian Foreign Minister. So he asked in what specific way the Soviets might be able to circumvent Brosak's botulin. 'As I have said, I don't know—'

'The botulin, yes. We understand it is already in position in your reservoirs.'

'Brosak said this?'

'Yes. Under...persuasion, yes. That much only.'

'But in that case—'

T M Voss held up a hand. 'We shall

find out more. From Brosak, who wishes to exterminate the Soviets and is willing to this end to exterminate your people if they do not concede defeat.' There was a pause. The people present, all of them except Brosak looking intently at Hedge, were very quiet and very still. There was no sound at all in the room. Hedge found it eerie; and alarming too. Again, perhaps, the psychological build-up, the prelude to disaster, possibly personal disaster. Then T M Voss went on: 'The President of the Supreme Soviet has himself personally spoken on the telephone to London. To the British Prime Minister herself. To tell her of our great concern for all your people who are under this wicked threat from a Nazi, a man who reveres the memory of a vile and evil person. Also to assure her of something else.'

'Yes?'

'To assure her that she has a representative in Moscow, a distinguished person from her Foreign Office, who will on her behalf and that of her government and Queen, assist in the smoothing out of all matters to ensure peace.'

Hedge could do nothing but gape.

'Who is this man, Roly?' Mrs Heffer had forgotten all about vanished Hedge.

Rowland Mayes blushed with embarrassed pleasure: back to Roly again. She needed him now; the Foreign Office was firmly back in the picture. He said, 'Hedge, Prime Minister?'

'You know who I'm talking about, Roly. *Is* he distinguished?'

'Not a word I would use, Prime Minister—'

Mrs Heffer looked impatient. 'Yes or no.'

'No.'

'Then can he be of any use?'

Rowland Mayes blew out a long breath. 'He may be, Prime Minister, and then again he may not. It's a debatable point. One that I'm really not able to give a very clear answer to.'

'So it would seem,' Mrs Heffer said. Rowland Mayes looked cowed. He'd spoken to the Permanent Under-Secretary about Hedge, and Hedge's suddenly revealed involvement, and the Permanent Under-Secretary had been dubious, to say the least, suggesting without actually saying so that Hedge might well have been responsible for the impasse so far and that if anyone could foul up a situation then that anyone was Hedge. Rowland Mayes prayed that Hedge would turn up trumps. If he didn't, then he, Rowland Mayes, would get the blame for that as well.

Mrs Heffer spoke again. 'Of course I made it *quite clear* to the Soviets that I would *not concede.*'

Rowland Mayes, wishing to clear up a point that he had hesitated to put until now, the last moment for peace as it were, but still knowing that he was on slippery ground, said diffidently, 'Prime Minister, there's just one thing.' He coughed.

'Yes?'

'The question of—of conceding. I'm unclear as to what you quite mean.'

Mrs Heffer stared. 'What I quite mean? I mean that I *won't concede*. Simply that.' Rowland Mayes ploughed on conscientiously. 'Concede what, Prime Minister? Concede to Brosak—*not* concede, I mean—or to the prospect of war?'

'What on earth are you talking about, Foreign Secretary?'

'There is surely a dichotomy, Prime Minister? As I'm sure you're aware—naturally you are—there is a feeling in the Cabinet that you're—well—prepared for war. If necessary, that is.' Rowland Mayes was twisting his body into a knot. 'The lesser, perhaps, of two evils. But is that not in fact conceding to Brosak? Of course I do realise that there's nothing—'

'For goodness sake, Foreign Secretary, as I've said before, if you cannot talk sense, shut up.'

Hedge was frozen with fear, with horror. He had to restrain himself from screaming, from uselessly attempting to run out of the dungeon to which, with Brosak, he had been taken. The dungeon was in the very bowels of the Lubyanka Prison, deep below the earth. Like the one he had been taken to earlier it was dank and smelled of torture, of humans put to the extremes of endurance, smelled of blood and urine and God alone knew what else. The thick stone walls were slimy and damp and mouldy and strange creatures crept upon the floor, white-looking slugs and worms and other denizens who had never known the light of day.

Foreign Minister T M Voss was there. So were a number of the armed guards, including the woman who had been one of Hedge's own escort earlier—how long ago now he couldn't have said. Four other men with the aspect of executioners were grouped around Brosak, who was lying prone upon a structure of heavy wood and metal, a structure that included a big wheel and a long metal pole with a thread like some gigantic screw. Brosak's shoulders were securely roped down to one end of the structure, his ankles to the other. There was an occasional squeak of machinery (it needed oiling) when the wheel was fractionally turned, and when the squeak came Brosak screamed and his body ran with sweat, clearly visible because he was naked.

Brosak was on a rack.

What primitive people, Hedge thought. This was right back to the Middle Ages and it was absolutely horrifying. Hedge could feel the dreadful rack pulling his own body apart and he quaked every time Brosak screamed.

It was, not unexpectedly, the gaunt man who was conducting the interrogation. He stood with the other two men at the feet end of the rack. 'Speak,' he said. 'About the botulin bags.'

Brosak's voice was now faint but high with pain. *'Heil Hitler,'* was all he said.

The gaunt man gestured to the men at Brosak's head and the big wheel was turned a little more. The squeak came and Brosak screamed as the metal pole's thread moved. The gaunt man was patient. 'Speak,' he said again. 'You know what we wish to know. How is the bagged botulin to be removed from the British reservoirs?'

There was no reply and the wheel was turned again.

Rowland Mayes was being deliberately tormented now. He realised that but knew that the Prime Minister was under very great strain and couldn't really be held responsible for her goading of him; basically she needed his support, his loyalty. So he put up with it when, having told him to shut up, she wouldn't let the matter drop.

'I prefer to leave it all to this man Sedge rather than you, if you can't co-operate sensibly, Foreign Secretary.'

'Hedge, Prime Minister, not—'

'That's what I *said*—Hedge. Do try to *listen.*'

'I'm sorry, Prime Minister.'

'A *deaf* Foreign Secretary's no use to anyone.'

Rowland Mayes fell silent. Mrs Heffer was a very difficult person to serve. A moment later she went to the security line, the one that connected her with Buckingham Palace. There was a pause while she waited for the instrument to be answered, then she spoke rather sharply. 'The Queen, please. And quickly. This is the Prime Minister.'

Mrs Heffer had barely finished briefing Her Majesty and not apparently listening to a word that was said to her in return when another of her battery of telephones rang. This was a further report from what she called the field. No more plastic bags. But at any moment they might become time-expired and shed their lethal contents. The matter was desperate, had really been desperate all along, but now it seemed more desperate because that man in Moscow was reported to be about to work miracles but evidently hadn't worked them yet. So near and yet so far, and already the element of surprise vis-à-vis the Russians had gone, or largely gone anyway—they might yet be lulled into a false sense of security because of the fact of their co-operation and it might be possible to make use of that. Suddenly Mrs Heffer brought herself up with a round turn. She had been brooding angrily on what Rowland Mayes had had the cheek to say about conceding and now she believed she had seen the point. What was the use, now, of attacking the Soviet?

None. Mrs Heffer scowled across her HQ.

Then another call came in. This time it was from Moscow. It was the Foreign Office man, the one whose name she simply *couldn't* remember.

Brosak, stretched to his limit—a hip bone had been pulled from its socket—had done his own conceding; he had agreed to speak. The wheel was at once turned the other way and Brosak, in response, seemed to sink back into himself, resuming more or less his normal length.

'Now speak,' the gaunt man said.

Brosak spoke; he spoke about the botulin and what he said didn't sound good. When he stopped speaking he was told to go on again. Instead of going on he cried. He cried like a child might for its mother. When he didn't stop crying the wheel was patiently turned again, the stretching way. Brosak stretched and screamed, and a whole leg came loose.

Hedge closed his eyes. He could take no more. But he couldn't shut his eyes to the screams. To his great relief the screams stopped and were replaced by a curious gurgling sound from Brosak's throat. A few seconds later Brosak died.

'Prime Minister, this is Hedge. In Moscow.' The line was pretty clear considering the distance and the fact that the call was coming from a country where everything mechanical and electrical was said to be continually breaking down. 'I have a report. The man Brosak, you know—'

'Yes. What is it?'

'Brosak has talked, Prime Minister. Unfortunately he's now dead—'

'Torture, one supposes.'

'Oh no, Prime Minister.' T M Voss had been adamant on this point and was currently listening in on the conversation on another telephone. 'Natural causes.'

'Well, never mind that, what did he say?'

'He revealed the whereabouts of the botulin bags, Prime Minister—'

'For heaven's sake, we *know that*. The reservoirs.'

'Yes—no—yes indeed, Prime Minister. The reservoirs, as you say. But only three of them, you see.'

'*Three* of them? What about the rest?'

'Bluff, Prime Minister,' Hedge said. 'In fact he considered three to be ample, quite sufficient to make, er, Britain give in to his demands—'

'Did he name the three?'

He named Siblyback and Ladybower—'

'Which we've found—the bags, I mean. *What* a relief! They must have been more accessible than he'd thought... What was that? Say again.'

Hedge said, 'Before he could name the third one, Prime Minister, he died.'

There was an impatient sound along the line. 'Damn the man. Where does *that* leave *us*, I'd like to know! Well?'

Hedge didn't answer that, having nothing to offer. But there was something he had to say, a very important point. 'Prime Minister, I have assured the President of the Supreme Soviet that there is now no longer any danger of an attack. No danger of war. He is immensely pleased to hear that. He was in fact ready to respond. In all respects. That, I have managed to avert. I trust I did right?'

Mrs Heffer paused before replying. She knew very well that the untrustworthy Russians would be listening in and she knew she had to be very, very careful—there was also the press and the electorate to be considered. Having thought deeply she said, *'Of course* you've done right. You've behaved *splendidly,* so *brave,* as *of course* one would expect of a Briton. I've had you in my *heartfelt prayers* all the time, Mr—' There was another pause, during which Hedge's ears caught the prompt of Rowland Mayes, 'Sedge. You have my *heartiest congratulations* on duty well and nobly done and you may be sure I shall bring your name to the attention of Her Majesty.' Hedge gave a great sigh of relief. Now he should be in the clear as regards the Russians, the Lubyanka, the gaunt man and both kinds of custody. He couldn't wait to see London again...then he remembered the kidnappers. They had wanted the delivery of Logan. Well, they couldn't have him now, of course. He hoped they would prove civilised enough to understand...

In Downing Street, Mrs Heffer had turned to the agog members of her Cabinet. 'You heard all that,' she said crisply. 'Of course, it was for the Russians' benefit. We're not out of the wood yet—but they did behave *splendidly* which is really quite astonishing for such barbarians. Now—a determined effort is to be made to find that remaining plastic bag. All police, all the armed forces, everybody. The public *everywhere* to continue taking full precautions until the thing's been found. Just the one—we shall prevail, I don't doubt that for *one moment.*'

She turned away to make one more telephone call, this time to Defence Ministry. She passed the word for the stand-down. The patrols, of strike aircraft and nuclear submarines, would continue as they had done around the clock day in, day out, year in, year out; the public would notice no difference. But now the word for the pressing of buttons would not go out.

The assembled ministers noticed a strange expression on Mrs Heffer's face as she made that call. It was a curious mixture of relief—tempered relief in the circumstances of one more bag—and intense disappointment that the Soviet Union would now go on being. But at least the election looked like being won.

When Shard returned to London and the FO he had a long yack with his DI.

'It's no use, Harry. You can't win. Not against the Hedges of this world.'

'I expect he gave them a load of old codswallop in Moscow. Right, sir?'

Shard grinned ruefully and sighed. 'Didn't do too brilliantly myself, did I? But I'm sure you're right. Whatever he told them or didn't tell them—he's due for the next Honours List.'

'You reckon?'

'Yes. And so, I'll bet, does Hedge.'

He went home to Ealing. He was dead tired; not much sleep for too long. Mrs Micklem was still in residence but was packing—he'd rung Beth as soon as he'd hit the UK from West Germany. Mrs Micklem gave him a sour look. 'Back again,' she said, with a hint of the bad penny in her tone. 'Missed all the bother, didn't you,' she went on. 'All that poison in the water—and we still don't know what's safe to drink. It's all right for some, Simon. Come back when it's all over.'

'Didn't you just suggest it's *not* all over yet, or did I mishear you, mother-in-law?'

He got a sharp look for that: she didn't

like it when he addressed her as mother-in-law since it carried certain quite decided undertones. 'There's no need to split hairs,' she said. 'Just like you, that is. I don't know how Beth puts up with it.'

Shard left it at that. There never was any point in arguing with Mrs Micklem. She always managed to twist things round her own way. Like Hedge.

The publishers hope that this book has
given you enjoyable reading. Large Print
Books are especially designed to be as easy
to see and hold as possible. If you want a
complete list of our books please ask
at your local library or write direct to:
Magna Large Print Books, Long Preston,
North Yorkshire, BD23 4ND, England.

This Large Print Book for the Partially sighted, who cannot read normal print, is published under the auspices of

THE ULVERSCROFT FOUNDATION

1	21	41	61	81	101	121	141	161	181
2	22	42	62	82	102	122	142	162	182
3	23	43	63	83	103	123	143	163	183
4	24	44	64	84	104	124	144	164	184
5	25	45	65	85	105	125	145	165	185
6	26	46	66	86	(106)	126	146	166	186
7	27	47	67	87	107	127	147	167	187
8	28	48	68	88	108	128	148	168	188
9	29	49	69	89	109	129	149	169	189
10	30	50	70	90	110	130	150	(170)	190
11	31	(51)	71	91	111	131	151	171	191
12	32	52	72	92	112	132	152	172	192
13	33	53	73	93	113	133	153	173	193
14	(34)	54	74	94	114	134	154	174	194
(15)	35	55	75	95	115	135	(155)	175	195
16	36	56	76	96	116	136	156	176	196
17	37	57	77	97	117	137	157	177	197
18	38	58	78	98	118	138	158	178	198
19	39	59	79	99	119	139	159	179	199
20	40	60	80	100	120	140	160	180	200

201	211	221	231	241	251	261	271	281	291
202	212	222	232	242	252	262	272	282	292
203	213	223	233	243	253	263	273	283	293
204	214	224	234	244	254	264	274	284	294
205	215	225	235	245	255	265	275	285	295
206	216	226	236	246	256	266	276	286	296
207	217	227	237	247	257	267	277	287	297
208	218	228	238	248	258	268	278	288	298
209	219	229	239	249	259	269	279	289	299
210	220	230	240	250	260	270	280	290	300

301	310	319	328	337	346
302	311	320	329	338	347
303	312	321	330	339	348
304	(313)	322	331	340	349
305	314	323	332	341	350
306	315	324	333	342	
307	316	325	334	343	
308	317	326	335	344	
309	318	327	336	345